I0452345

BROKEN CHAIN

BY LISA VON BIELA

Paul crouched in the straw next to a downer cow. But there was something odd about the animal. Instead of thrashing and foaming and fighting whatever ailed her, she simply lay there, quiet and still. As if she'd gone beyond caring. Something about it gave Les a strange feeling.

He stepped into the stall and approached the cow for a closer look. When he saw her, he couldn't believe Paul would've spent the money to have him come out.

"Well, Paul, why'd you call me out here for this?" He motioned toward the cow. "It's just old age. Nothing invented can cure that."

Paul looked up at him with weary eyes. "That's the thing of it, Doc. She's not. She's only a year old, but she looks like an old, used-up cow."

Les opened his mouth, but didn't quite know what to say. He glanced down at the cow again. The fur, brittle and dull. The eyes, bloodshot. Cloudy lenses pregnant with cataract. An old cow. He lifted her lip to look at the teeth and was stunned. The teeth showed minimal wear—like those of a yearling. He sat back on his heels in the straw and ran through his mental list of diseases, which, after all his years in practice, was pretty damned encyclopedic. And he came up empty.

"Never seen anything like it, Paul."

"Me neither, that's for sure."

"Is this the only one, or have there been others? When did you first notice this?"

"Only noticed it in the past few weeks, maybe couple of months. At first I just thought I had a couple of random deaths. But then I started paying closer attention, and the thing they have in common is they all look like they're dying of old age, but they're not old. I don't know what to make of it, and I sure as shit can't afford to have this happening." He rubbed his jaw with a trembling hand.

For David, with love

CHAPTER 1

Dustin Lyons was not where he was supposed to be at six o'clock that morning.

Carrie Lyons pounded her fist on the open barn door, rattling its tired, rusty hinges. "Dustin! Where the hell are you? Your breakfast is getting cold and you *know* I need to go open up the café." She slapped the overhead light switch and froze in her tracks when she saw what lurked inside.

Snarling, Dustin crouched by the hay bales like a crazed animal. With his wild eyes and matted hair, he looked just like one of those meth-heads on the billboards out by the highway. But Dustin didn't take meth, or any other illegal drugs. In all of their twenty years of marriage, the worst he'd done is have a little too much whiskey on a Saturday night. He never got like this. Never.

"What is the *matter* with you?" Carrie took a few uncertain steps forward to get a better look.

He stared right at her with those savage eyes, then grabbed a hay hook and started swinging it—*hard*—from side to side. Carrie gasped and took a step back. Dustin leaped up from his crouch, slashing this way and that with the sharp, treacherous hook. He bared his clenched teeth and let out a growl as he started toward her.

"Dustin—" Heart pounding, Carrie held out her hands and took another step back, unable to accept the sight of her own husband looking like a madman. There had to be an explanation, had to be a solution—something that would get him to snap back to his normal self. But she was damned if she could think of it right now.

Dustin clutched the gleaming metal hook in both hands, raised it high, and lunged. Carrie screamed and turned to make a run for the door, but her work boot slipped. She slammed flat down on her stomach, knocking the wind out of her lungs and stunning herself for just a tick too long.

The hay hook got her just under her back rib cage, sliding in with remarkable ease, smooth as butter. She marveled at this in the heartbeat moment before the pain came. Then the hook forged a searing line of agony from her skin all the way inside to whatever organs it ruined.

Dustin flipped her onto her side with the hook as easily as he would have shifted a bale of hay. Then he ripped the bloody blade back out and stared down at her with hateful eyes. She couldn't tell if he even knew who she was.

Then he brought down his weapon, over and over again, until the darkness came and delivered her from the pain of the hook—and from the pain of seeing her Dustin transformed into some kind of killing monster.

CHAPTER 2

"**O**w!" Gretchen Sommers sucked on her finger to quell the sting from the hot oil spatter that had just nailed her, then yanked open the kitchen drawer next to the stove. They'd moved into the cramped little apartment in such a low-budget rush that she couldn't remember where half their stuff was. She rummaged through the drawer's contents, utensils clattering, until she found the nylon spatula she wanted. She huffed, then stirred the ground beef as it sizzled and browned in the pan. When the macaroni was done, she'd throw it together with the beef and a jar of spaghetti sauce and serve up her family's favorite comfort food. Maybe that would help them all feel a little more settled in their new surroundings.

Everything made her feel closed in right now. Their dinky kitchen in their equally dinky apartment. Their shoestring budget. Their sketchy neighborhood. The crappy air conditioning that was no match for the nasty, sticky heat of Washington, D.C., in July. She absently rubbed her belly. About the only thing letting up for the moment was her morning sickness as she entered her second trimester.

At least food had started appealing to her again. She scooped up a mouthful of the partially cooked ground beef with her spatula, blew on it briefly, and then popped it into her mouth. She loved the taste of the meat itself without the distractions of the sauce and pasta. She inhaled, savoring the smell of the cooking beef, and stirred the macaroni once again to keep it from sticking.

Gretchen leaned back against the counter, swiped a trickle

of sweat from her forehead, and sighed. Things were tough now, uprooting themselves as they had, but it would be worth it in the end. Kyle had done well in his clinical training at the University of Minnesota Med School. He'd found himself particularly drawn to epidemiology, so he was elated to be accepted into the CDC's two-year Epidemic Intelligence Service program, or EIS for short. As a "disease detective," he'd be sent out on assignments to track down the sources of various epidemics. And when he completed the elite program, he'd have a great career ahead of him in epidemiology.

That was the story—on paper, anyway. Gretchen wondered what their life would actually be like over the next two years. Kyle would surely be completely consumed with his work, as he had been during his medical training so far. She'd be busy caring for little Lara, now three and extremely active and precocious, as well as little No-Name, currently incubating inside her. That much she did know. But what would his assignments be like? Would he be away for long periods at a time?

She shrugged and stirred the beef. She'd just have to roll with it, hard as it was for her. She already missed her job managing the emergency food shelf and shelter programs at HopeShare. But she loved Kyle, and knew he'd make a terrific doctor, so she'd do whatever it took to let him focus on his training. Once he started practicing medicine, she'd find another job like she had at HopeShare, and everything would fall into place.

Lara trotted into the kitchen with her curly blonde hair framing her face like a halo and her tiny bare feet slapping on the linoleum. She clutched her favorite toy, her omnipresent stuffed sheep, Baa-Baa. "When's dinner, Mommy? I'm hungry and so is Daddy!"

Gretchen smiled. Even the stress and disruption of the move couldn't shake her love for that little girl. So perfect and so precious. And to think they'd nearly lost her. Born prematurely, she'd spent the first two months of her life in the hospital, fighting to survive. The doctors couldn't explain why it happened, so no matter how hard she tried not to think about it, every single day she worried it could happen again with this pregnancy.

She bent, picked Lara up and hoisted her and Baa-Baa onto her hip. "Dinner's coming soon, honey. See?" She pointed toward the range top.

Lara smiled and giggled. "Woot, Mommy! Dinner!"

Kyle pushed aside his plate on the Formica kitchen table, leaned back in the thinly padded vinyl chair, and smiled. "Thanks for making that tonight. Reminds me of home, back in Minnesota."

He glanced around their apartment and marveled at how little your money bought out in this neck of the woods. The place was small, worn, and in the sort of neighborhood that wasn't safe for long walks—even before the wave of violence that had been spreading across the country like an epidemic. But it was what they could afford and it wasn't that far from his office. Plus it was right on the Metro line, so he could skip the nasty D.C. traffic.

"You know, I already miss Minnesota. D.C. isn't my kind of place. If it weren't for the EIS position …"

Gretchen reached over and put her hand on his forearm. "I miss it, too. But it's the only way for you to get this training, so we'll just have to manage for a couple of years. Then we can go pretty much wherever we want, right?"

"That's the plan. Once I graduate, we can settle down someplace nice to raise the kids. Bet we could go back to Minnesota if we wanted." He turned to Lara, who'd managed to spread a good portion of her dinner across her face. Amazing the kid actually got any nutrition. "Where do *you* want to live when I'm done?"

Lara considered the question for a moment, her deep blue eyes trained on the ceiling as she appeared to sort through a range of possibilities in her head. Then she clapped her hands together and proclaimed, "Disneyland!"

Kyle ruffled her curly hair. "Why doesn't that surprise me?" He glanced at the clock on the range hood. "Hey, what do you say we watch a little news, then make it an early night? I want to be well rested for my first day tomorrow."

"Sure, go ahead with Lara. I'll be there soon as I clear the dishes."

"Thanks." He grabbed a couple of paper napkins. "Let's get you cleaned up first so your dinner doesn't end up all over the furniture." He daubed at Lara's sauce-laden face while she squirmed in mock protest and giggled.

"All clean now, Daddy?"

"Yep, looking good."

He helped her down from her chair and she ran into the adjoining room, Baa-Baa tucked tightly under her arm. He joined her on the coach and turned on the TV.

Lara rubbed her eyes. "What's that?"

"The news. Just for a few minutes, then we'll all go to bed."

"Boring," she announced with a yawn. Apparently uninterested in the day's events, she curled up with Baa-Baa and closed her eyes.

Kyle lowered the volume so she could fall asleep.

Not again, he thought as the lead story came on.

"*The unprecedented number of seemingly random acts of violence continues to mount. As we've reported in the past several months, these incidents are not limited to densely populated areas with traditionally higher crime rates. They're also occurring in locales with normally low rates of violence—and they're increasing in overall frequency.*

"*One incident reported today occurred in a small town in southcentral Minnesota: St. Joseph, in Sibley County. Dustin Lyons, a longtime resident and farmer with no prior history of violence or any brushes with the law brutally attacked and killed his wife of twenty years, Carrie Lyons, with a hay hook, and then apparently took his own life with the same hook. A neighbor happened to stop in shortly after the incident and found the bodies.*"

Kyle grabbed the remote and clicked off the TV. St. Joe wasn't that far from where he'd grown up. It was a peaceful little farming community where everyone knew each other pretty well and would always band together to help out if someone was struggling. That guy must have snapped without any warning or someone would have intervened before it got to the point where he would do something like that.

The epidemic of violence worried him more each day. And now they'd moved to a densely populated place with a high crime rate that looked like it would only get worse. He glanced down at Lara's peaceful, sleeping face and hoped he hadn't endangered his family by accepting the EIS position.

CHAPTER 3

Marty Janssen grabbed the wooden fence post and gave it a good, strong tug. Solid. He stepped back, took off his baseball cap, wiped sweat from his brow with the back of his wrist, and put the cap back on. He stood in the heat of the mid-day sun, hands on hips, and gazed out at his farm. The pasture grass had that deep green typical of a Minnesota midsummer. The winters locked you up like a bitch in these parts, but the spring and summer still held a beauty that never grew old for him.

His herd of Black Angus dotted the lush green of the pasture, creating a scene like something from a picture postcard. To the casual observer, it undoubtedly looked like a peaceful existence. But after working the farm alone for most of his adult life, Marty knew nothing could be further from the truth.

The weather could betray you at any time. Too wet. Too dry. Too violent with the periodic hail storm, or, God forbid, the occasional tornado passing through. Prices could screw you, too—oversupply could kill commodity prices, making the difference some years between a modest profit and a devastating loss. Huge corporate farms made the problem worse with their mass-production methods that kept commodity prices artificially low.

And then the animals themselves, for livestock producers like him. Despite all the available vaccinations and antibiotics, a bug could run right through a herd. Even if it didn't kill individual animals, it could retard their growth, make 'em light when they went to market. Fewer pounds, fewer dollars.

Marty squinted against the sun and stared at his herd. He'd

lost a few lately. He didn't know why, and that bothered him. Never saw anything like it before, and didn't quite know how to describe the problem to the vet. The animals that died hadn't seemed sick, not really. They'd just died. That's it. No symptoms typical of any disease, and he'd seen plenty over the years. It was like they'd just finished living before their time, and that was that.

He slapped a mosquito on his neck and was about to go inside for some lunch when his cell rang. He took it out of his pocket and looked at the screen. Paul Gorsham from the farm next to his. He answered the call.

"Hey, Paul, what's up?"

"Hi, Marty. Just finished some repairs on my irrigation pipes. Never ends, you know?"

"True enough. Just finished fixing a couple of loose fence posts myself. Wouldn't be quite so bad if we didn't have to get all the year's repairs done in the few months with decent weather."

"Yeah, that and having to do it all myself. Haven't been able to afford to hire any help the last few years. Don't know what I'm going to do when my arthritis gets bad enough that I can't do it myself anymore."

Marty fell silent. Paul's remark hit on one of his own big worries. His wife Ellen had died years ago, and the kids had long since moved away. They had zero interest in staying on with the family farm, and had gone on to desk jobs in the city. He, too, hadn't been able to afford help the last few years and it was a matter of time before the maintenance and daily work became too much for him. He had no idea what he was going to do when that day came, and he didn't want to think about it right now.

"So, Paul, what'd you call about?"

"Oh, I was wondering what you thought about what happened on the Lyons farm the other day."

"I tell ya, I don't know what to make of it. Dustin was a good man." He shook his head. "He was just over here last week to return a power saw he'd borrowed. He seemed perfectly fine."

"I saw him and Carrie pretty recently myself. Nothing out of the ordinary at all. Never saw anything like this coming—not out here in St. Joe, and certainly not out of Dustin. Of course, with all the violence going on everywhere, maybe we shouldn't be surprised it's happening here, too."

"I *hope* this isn't related to what's been on the news. Maybe he had a brain tumor or something that made him do it. I suppose it doesn't matter in the end, though. Won't bring him or Carrie back."

"Yeah. I'm worried about what'll happen to his farm, too. I'd hate to see it gobbled up by BigAg, but you know that's what'll happen if their kids don't come back to run it. It'll get foreclosed on and some big outfit'll snap it up for pennies on the dollar. That'd make the whole thing doubly tragic."

"Those big operations're getting too close for comfort as it is. Here in St. Joe anyway, we've managed to hold on to the family farms. For now. Something like this could help 'em get a toehold in here." Marty cleared his throat. "Well, I gotta get going. More stuff to do before the day ends."

"Yeah, sure. Take care, Marty."

"You, too. Bye."

Marty slipped his phone back into his pocket and frowned. He didn't much like it when things happened without explanation. Why the hell would a guy like Dustin do what they say he did? He didn't want to believe that crazy big-city violence was coming to his quiet little town. Like he didn't have enough to worry about. He gazed out over his pasture and wondered how much longer he could hold on to his farm.

Shoulders slumped, he turned and started walking back toward the house, then decided to visit Ellen. Her grave, covered in wildflowers and surrounded by a low, black, wrought-iron fence, lay beneath a tall maple in the backyard. The little gate squealed as he swung it open. He stepped inside, knelt on one knee beside her tombstone, then traced the letters of her name with his finger. *Ellen Leanne Janssen.*

"Wish you were still here … I miss you so much." He wiped a tear from his eye and stood. No matter how often he visited her, the pain never lessened. He expected it never would. Marty sighed and stepped away from the grave, shutting the little gate behind him.

Maybe he'd be able to shake the dark thoughts from his mind with a decent lunch. And perhaps a little shot of bourbon.

CHAPTER 4

Daphne Mercer twisted the box fan's knob to High, then got back to work scrubbing the grill as if her life depended on it. She'd run the AC soon enough when she opened the café. For now, she was in penny-pinching mode. If she could cut her power bill even a little by using the fan in the meantime, she would.

It's not like she wasn't used to humid Minnesota summers. She was born and raised in the Twin Cities, though until recently she'd spent most of her time in air-conditioned office or restaurant jobs. But she'd never felt that she fit in there. When both her thirtieth birthday and a nasty breakup with her longtime boyfriend slammed her in the face, she took stock of her life and decided she didn't like what she saw.

She took no joy in the daily grind and trying to compete with people she felt were more set on status than values. She'd grown to hate the crowded, rushed feel of the city and the traffic. Not to mention the rising tide of violence. Not a day went by without some shooting or stabbing, and the rate of incidents had been increasing of late with frightening regularity.

Life was too short to waste. She needed to simplify her life, get back to what was important to her, and find a safer place to live. So she decided to set herself up in small-town rural Minnesota.

Daphne had worked long enough in restaurants as a waitperson—even a cook—that she figured she knew enough to run a small café. So she took a long drive one weekend earlier that summer through some beautiful farm country southwest of the Cities and stumbled across St. Joe. It looked like a Norman Rockwell painting to her, with its little town square full of small businesses and its surrounding expanse of open ag land.

She'd noticed a closed café right on the town square with a For Rent sign in the window. The realtor handling it told her a woman named Carrie Lyons had been renting the space to run her café, but that she'd died recently. The owner needed a new tenant, and so she'd come along at the perfect time. The space already contained the needed equipment and fixtures. All she had to do was personalize it to suit her own taste.

Daphne couldn't believe her luck. She'd put down a deposit on the spot, received her key, and rented a room for herself and her cat Agnes at the motel-apartment combination the next block over. No more commute, no more dumb bosses trying to tell her what to do.

In the last couple of weeks, she'd worked harder than ever before to bring her dream to life. The place hadn't been left in the best condition. Dust covered every surface, and she couldn't have that. The bare picture windows made it look like a truck stop, so she put up some nice white lace curtains to soften the café's appearance and make it look homey. She put lace tablecloths and glass vases with silk flowers on each table to create a little atmosphere.

But the worst thing was the grease. Ms. Lyons had apparently been a big believer in the meaty and the fried. Probably what killed the poor woman. The grill was caked with it. Daphne was amazed it passed health inspections, it was so bad. The grease had built up along the edges of every single surface in the kitchen—in the fan vents, on the walls, and for good measure, it had even formed a thick and rancid patina on the grill's main cooking surface.

She wrinkled her nose as she thought of the massive amount of animal fat that must have passed through the cooking area while Ms. Lyons had run the place. Well, those days were over. Nothing but good soy oil and meat substitutes from now on. She'd have some dairy and egg dishes for the lacto- and ovo-vegetarians. She'd have soy-based products for the strict vegans. Yep, she'd serve nothing but the healthy stuff in *her* café, like she'd been eating for years now. Vegetarian foods, fresh fruits and vegetables.

That whole Mad Cow thing had made her think when the

story first broke some time back, and she'd left the meat world—beef, poultry, and pork alike—behind and never looked back. She smiled as she examined the grill's clean, shiny surface—the product of hours and hours of scrubbing and hard work. She envisioned how proud and happy she would be to make her living running a bustling small-town café of her own.

CHAPTER 5

L es Anderson turned his truck onto Paul Gorsham's familiar farm property, drove up the long dirt driveway, and parked in his usual spot near the house. In all his thirty-one years of veterinary practice, he'd never heard a story like Paul had told him when he called to make an appointment. He shook his head and wondered if Paul had taken leave of his senses or if something truly new was afoot.

He was still sitting in his truck, pondering the reason for his visit, when Paul's wife Susan emerged from the house, wiping her hands on a dish towel. She came up to the driver's side of the truck as Les lowered the window.

"Hi, Susan. How've you been?"

"Good, thanks, but Paul's pretty worried about some of the stock."

"That's what he was telling me. Sounded kind of odd."

"Oh, it is. You'll see." She pointed toward the barn. "You'll find him in there. Good to see you again, Les." She smiled and headed back to the house as if she had plenty to do.

Les watched her go. Not for the first time, he wondered what his life would have been like if he'd made different choices. He'd had a huge crush on Susan back in high school but, for reasons he found inconsequential in retrospect, had asked someone else to the senior prom. Paul asked Susan to the prom, and they'd been together ever since. He'd eventually ended up with Tammie, who'd decided pretty quickly she didn't much appreciate sharing the life of a country vet, with the midnight calls for calving and the stink of his clothes from manure and other things.

He didn't miss Tammie so much as he wished he'd done things differently and ended up with Susan. She was still a beautiful woman, even after all these years. Slender, but strong and healthy-looking. Her hair had grayed, but it had turned that vibrant shade of gray that actually looked really pretty on her. He shook his head, grabbed his bag, and headed over to the barn to see what Paul was so worried about.

He knocked on the barn door. "Hey Paul, it's me, Les."

"Over here, last stall in the back."

Les entered the barn and let his eyes adjust for a few moments. The July sun left him temporarily helpless inside the dimly light structure, reminding him he had to check with the eye doctor about those cataracts. Then he walked over to the back stall.

Paul crouched in the straw next to a downer cow. But there was something odd about the animal. Instead of thrashing and foaming and fighting whatever ailed her, she simply lay there, quiet and still. As if she'd gone beyond caring. Something about it gave Les a strange feeling.

He stepped into the stall and approached the cow for a closer look. When he saw her, he couldn't believe Paul would've spent the money to have him come out.

"Well, Paul, why'd you call me out here for this?" He motioned toward the cow. "It's just old age. Nothing invented can cure that."

Paul looked up at him with weary eyes. "That's the thing of it, Doc. She's not. She's only a year old, but she *looks* like an old, used-up cow."

Les opened his mouth, but didn't quite know what to say. He glanced down at the cow again. The fur, brittle and dull. The eyes, bloodshot. Cloudy lenses pregnant with cataract. An old cow. He lifted her lip to look at the teeth and was stunned. The teeth showed minimal wear—like those of a yearling. He sat back on his heels in the straw and ran through his mental list of diseases, which, after all his years in practice, was pretty damned encyclopedic. And he came up empty.

"Never seen anything like it, Paul."

"Me neither, that's for sure."

"Is this the only one, or have there been others? When did you first notice this?"

"Only noticed it in the past few weeks, maybe couple of months. At first I just thought I had a couple of random deaths. But then I started paying closer attention, and the thing they have in common is they all look like they're dying of old age, but they're not old. I don't know what to make of it, and I sure as shit can't afford to have this happening." He rubbed his jaw with a trembling hand.

Les put his hand out to try to calm Paul. "I hear ya, I do. I just have no ready answer." He glanced down again at the cow, searching for clues and finding none. "I'm going to have to look into this some more. Keep me posted on what happens with this one, how long it takes. I'll want to do a post on her immediately after death."

"But she's—"

"I know. Normally I'd put her out of her misery, but I don't want to introduce anything that might skew the lab results." Les stood and stretched his lower back. "This is odd, indeed, and I want to try to get to the bottom of it as quickly as I can."

CHAPTER 6

Vic Rayburn was a man who enjoyed his job. As head of the EIS, the CDC's Epidemic Intelligence Service, each year he got to handpick a new crop of the most promising future epidemiologists available. As he sat at his desk and scrolled through the roster of this year's cohort on his computer, he marveled at how he'd been able to select better and better candidates each year. The real-world experience they would get in the program would mold them into experts who would be in high demand for their skills. He smiled. He was proud of his program's graduates and what they would surely achieve during their careers.

Now that the new cohort had completed orientation, it was time to start assigning them to their initial projects. Vic always took care to fit the assignment to the individual's particular interests or background. He pulled up the list of current potential outbreaks from the real-time database and began to comb through it for candidate assignments.

In his own career as a practicing epidemiologist, Vic had developed an enviable sixth sense about trends, often correctly identifying a nascent epidemic long before his colleagues. He'd begun to suspect an epidemiologic basis behind the massive uptick in violence—something more than socioeconomic factors—and so he'd been gathering raw data into his database for the past several weeks.

He clicked a link in the report to access more detail, then scanned the various charts and graphs with a practiced eye. Viewing the trend over time, the violence appeared to have originated in the Midwest, then bloomed out across the country in all directions, seeming to follow major distribution routes.

It affected both densely and sparsely populated areas, urban and rural. The violence was of all kinds: shootings, stabbings, poisonings, you name it. So it wasn't as if access to a particular type of weapon created any pattern.

Vic sat back in his chair and frowned. In fact, he'd recently heard a rather grisly report of a man killing his wife—and then himself—with a hay hook out in Minnesota somewhere. The problem appeared to be writ both large and small: impersonal mass shootings and personal, gruesome murders like that one.

He accessed the news story on that incident and confirmed the details. The small town where it happened was near Minneapolis. He was almost certain one of the new recruits was from somewhere around there. A quick search of the cohort list showed that Kyle Sommers was from the area, and had attended med school at the U of M, in fact. He sent an email to Kyle to meet with him in an hour.

Judging from the available data, Vic believed the violence would likely get far worse in the coming weeks and months, and that the root cause would be extremely difficult to pin down. He decided to give the project top priority, and to assemble a large team to investigate the problem from different angles and in different environments across the country. Some, like Kyle, would be placed in smaller rural locales, and some would be placed in more densely populated urban locales. That approach would be more likely to highlight patterns that cut across different environments than a single-site investigation, and so might lead to the true answer faster.

Good. One project decided. Vic rubbed his hands together and started selecting the rest of the team members.

CHAPTER 7

Gretchen lay draped on the couch, feet propped up on the coffee table, head lolled back. She fanned herself with a section of newspaper while Lara played with Baa-Baa on the floor, seemingly oblivious to the stifling heat. She wondered how crappy their AC unit must be if it couldn't cool the air in such a small space as their apartment.

A sheen of oily sweat covered her entire body, causing her T-shirt and shorts to cling to her in a disgusting, annoying way. The oppressive heat and sticky clothes only served to aggravate her morning sickness, just when she thought she was moving out of that miserable phase of her pregnancy. *Bonus*, she thought.

Lara hopped up with the boundless energy of a three-year-old when the door opened and Kyle walked in. "Woot! It's Daddy!" She ran to him and wrapped her arms around his left knee. He reached down and picked her up.

"Are you okay? You look like you've melted into the couch."

"The AC is a piece of crap. It's been stifling in here all day, and I dare not open the window. It's even worse outside."

Kyle smiled as Lara showered him with welcome-home kisses. "Well, never fear. We're going to leave it all behind."

Gretchen dropped her newspaper and sat up. "We just got here. Did something happen?"

"Got my first assignment." Kyle sat down next to Gretchen and let Lara jump out of his lap to go play with her stuffed sheep. "I'm part of a big team that's been assembled to investigate the wave of violence. Pretty important assignment out of the gate, if you ask me."

"Wow! When? And where?"

"Soon as I can start. Vic Rayburn—he runs the program—thinks there's an epidemiological basis to the violence, and that it's going to get a lot worse. So he's putting investigators in a bunch of different cities, some small, some large."

"How's that supposed to work?"

"We'll all manage our own investigations remotely in our assigned locations, and communicate via email and regular phone conferences. He thinks if he put the entire team in one location, we might see things as patterns that aren't really patterns. So because the problem cuts across urban and rural locations, he wants the investigation to do so as well."

"Oh, I see. You didn't say where yet."

"Back near Minneapolis. In a little farming town called St. Joseph, in Sibley County. It's a good setup, I think. Small enough scale for me to manage my first investigation, and near enough to St. Paul so I can pretty easily get out to meet with the state epidemiologist as needed."

"Oh. Do you know how long you'll be out there?" The thought of life without Kyle in the vile apartment wasn't pretty.

"No, but Vic projected it would be long enough that you and Lara can come with me."

"What about our stuff?"

"He suggested we just move into one of those extended-stay hotels the next town over, at least for now. If it gets more long-term, maybe we make other arrangements. I'm in the program for two years, so I'll have other assignments over time. Makes sense to leave this as our base of operations, since I can't predict where my future assignments will be."

Gretchen steepled her hands together and held them over her mouth as she absorbed Kyle's news. The move to D.C. had been enough of a hassle that she didn't want to repeat the process anytime soon—but, she hadn't exactly enjoyed their brief time there. July in D.C. in a lousy neighborhood was pretty much her vision of hell. Despite how simple Kyle made it sound, though, her head already spun with logistics. Depending how long the assignment lasted, she might have to find a local OB/GYN to monitor her pregnancy, maybe even her delivery. She rubbed her face and took a deep breath. She'd deal with all that in due time. At least they'd be back in their home state for a while.

"Are you okay with this? I figured you and Lara'd rather be out there with me than sitting here, so I cleared it with Vic."

Gretchen turned and gripped Kyle in a tight hug. "Of course we would. It'll be an adventure, certainly better than hanging around here without you. I'm so proud of you. I just hope there *is* some underlying cause that can be addressed."

"I hope so, too. And if there is, I hope I can find it. It's a really unusual sort of epidemic to investigate. On one hand, I'm excited to get this as my first assignment, but I'm sure it's going to be a really tough one."

Gretchen nuzzled her face into his shoulder. "We'll get through it together. We've gotten this far through med school, we can get through this and you're going to do a great job, I know. This assignment will open all kinds of doors for you."

CHAPTER 8

Cindy Morrow couldn't believe their luck. She and her bestie Sarah Donahue had managed to arrive at the Blue Moon in time to snag a table for two right up next to the stage, where their favorite local rock band, Dangerbus, would be playing shortly. The Blue Moon was a dinky old spot—just a bar, some plain old-school wooden tables and chairs, the stage, and a little space for dancing. Dangerbus was überpopular and the place would likely be standing-room-only pretty soon.

She glanced at her watch. "Should be on anytime now. This is going to be soooo awesome!"

Sarah lit a cigarette, took a deep drag, then blew a column of smoke up into the cloud that hung over the entire dimly lit room. "They're always awesome. Remember when they played the Tavern a couple months back? Great show. I could've listened to them all night." She downed the last of her third margarita and signaled the server for another.

Cindy hoped Sarah would last the evening. To get the coveted table, they'd arrived a couple of hours early. With not much else to do but drink and fend off unwanted advances, they'd already had a few, as the slight glassiness in Sarah's eyes attested. She took a cautious sip of her third glass of chardonnay. "I can't wait to see Ian North play. He's so freakin' hot."

Sarah laughed the low chuckle of a veteran smoker and smiled. "Yeah, what's not to like about him? He can sure rock a pair of leather pants, and how he can make his guitar do what it does, well …" She took another drag of her cigarette, licked her lips with exaggerated gusto, and fanned herself with a cocktail napkin.

Cindy sat back in her hard wooden chair and observed her friend. They'd known each other since high school, and had been hitting the singles scene together all through college and now into their late twenties. Neither of them'd had a relationship with a man last for very long, and sometimes Cindy wondered if that might be significant. Sarah was, after all, drop-dead gorgeous. She had the tall, graceful good looks of Angelina Jolie, but with a healthier bit of meat on her bones. Maybe they should at least have a conversation sometime about … possibilities.

Two fresh drinks appeared on their table just as a man's voice blasted out from the PA system.

"And now, put your hands together for … Dangerbus!"

A deafening roar erupted as everyone began applauding wildly and hooting. Reddish lights lit the stage, with a single white spotlight trained on the center. The all-male band, every one of them shirtless and clad in tight black leather pants, came out and took their places. Ian North stepped into the spotlight with his guitar and approached the mike. "How're ya doin' tonight? Are ya ready to rock?"

Amid cheers and screams from the audience, Ian positioned his guitar, then swung his arm down and nailed a chord so loud it threatened to split every eardrum in the place. The rest of the band joined in, and the walls struggled to contain the blasting rock music.

Consumed by the blaring beat, Cindy tapped her feet and jiggled in her chair as Dangerbus gave its audience what they'd come for. She knew her ears would ring for days after this, but she didn't care about that right now. She gulped some more of her wine and glanced over at her friend. Sarah leaned forward, elbows on the table, alternating puffs on her cigarette with sips of her drink. Cindy loved how she looked so focused on the music, and probably on Ian as well.

Sarah suddenly sat straight up and turned to Cindy with an alarmed look on her face. "Did you see that?" she mouthed.

"What?"

"Ian. Something weird just happened." She shouted to be heard above the music.

Cindy glanced back up at the stage. Something did look

slightly off with Ian. He'd stepped back toward the rear of the stage and stood with his guitar hanging at his side. In the relative gloom outside the spotlight, he appeared to have a confused look on his face.

"I don't know. Something's not right. Why isn't he playing?"

Sarah shook her head and leaned close to Cindy to be better heard. "It's like the rest of the band didn't notice or doesn't care. He has a major solo in this song. Maybe he's going to do it different this time."

As Cindy watched, Ian staggered back into the spotlight. He held the guitar by its neck with one hand, and raised his other hand to rub his eyes. When he moved his hand away from his face, his eyes widened as if he'd just realized where he was. For just a moment, he looked frightened, glancing around the room, then at the rest of the band. The other band members finally noticed his behavior and came to a discordant halt.

In the sudden silence, Ian opened his mouth wide and let out a scream that seemed to come from the darkest depths imaginable. Then he took hold of the guitar neck in both hands, swung it around, and smashed it to pieces on the keyboardist's head. The keyboardist crumpled to the floor beneath his instrument and the rest of the band fled backstage. Ian then grabbed the metal mike stand and yanked at it until he broke it free of its power cable.

Cindy glanced at Sarah, who sat openmouthed and frozen in place. "What the fuck?" Then she glanced back at the stage and regretted their choice of table.

Mike stand held aloft, Ian nimbly leaped down from the stage and before either Cindy or Sarah could react, he swung the stand at them like a baseball bat.

The last thing Cindy would ever see was the glint of light on the silver of the stand, right before it smashed into her temple and shattered her skull.

CHAPTER 9

Kyle pushed the spiral notebook to one side of his work desk, then flexed the day's tension from his shoulders. He glanced around the makeshift field office he'd set up in their extended-stay room. A laptop, a small printer/scanner, and a nice high-speed Internet connection. The setup was comfortable and efficient. His only concern was that it might be hard to concentrate when Lara was awake and playing, but he'd likely spend most of his time in the field anyway. He could do the desk work when she was in bed if he had to.

The two-bedroom suite was much nicer than their D.C. apartment, and the area—though not untouched by violence— would at least be somewhat safer for Gretchen and Lara. The location was perfect for his work, too. Gaylord was the county seat, so he'd have convenient access to county offices, like that of the public health director, Sherry Nelson. It was only about sixty miles to the capitol, so he would easily be able to arrange meetings with the state epidemiologist, Dr. Fred McKinsey. And of course, it was only minutes from St. Joe.

Gretchen came over and gave him a gentle hug from behind. "How's it going?" He reached back and gave her hand a squeeze.

"So far, so good. I've figured out the key contacts I need to make, where the hospitals and clinics are located, and I've sketched out my first steps."

"That didn't take long. We've only been here a couple days."

"Can't afford for it to take long. I expect this to be tough to chase down, so I need to get busy right out of the gate." He swiveled his chair to face her. "So what do you think of the place?"

She swept a blonde curl out of her eye. "It's nice. Well-equipped and comfortable. Of course I'm going to have to scope out the town pretty soon. Right now, I only know where the grocery store is." She smiled. "I'm glad we got the second rental car. Gaylord is small for a county seat, but it's not like everything's walking distance."

"I'm not sure I'd want you walking everywhere anyway. This isn't D.C., but I wouldn't be here if there weren't problems. Plus, I'll be driving around a lot. One car would've left you two stranded in the room all the time. Can't have that."

"No, we can't. Lara would go nuts sitting around here, even if I didn't. Hey, are you about done for the day? Do you want dinner now?"

"Yeah, I'd like to make it an early evening, so I can hit the ground running tomorrow."

Gretchen put the last of the morning's dishes into the dishwasher and shut its door. She gazed out the kitchen window at the landscaped courtyard one story below. Though the place was remarkably homey for a hotel, she still felt displaced. No doubt it had to do with their rushed move to D.C., then coming here, also seemingly overnight. All that combined with the erratic hormones of early pregnancy. She shrugged. *No wonder.*

"Hey Lara, let's go to the other room now." She bent down and picked up the child, who'd been happily busying herself with Baa-Baa in the middle of the kitchen floor.

"Cartoons, Mommy?" She grinned. "Woot!"

Not for the first time, Gretchen was thankful Lara was such an easy child to care for. Even when she'd turned two, she'd had none of the little monster persona that can inhabit kids of that age. She glanced at Kyle's work area as she passed by it with Lara balanced on her hip. He'd taken his laptop with him, as well as one of the notebooks. Even so, it still looked like a miniature nerve center with the books, bulletin board, and whiteboard he'd set up. *Organization* was that man's middle name.

She sat Lara on the couch beside her and turned on the TV, looking for cartoons. She found something suitable after a few channel clicks and Lara sat back with her sheep, mesmerized.

Gretchen leaned her elbow on the arm of the couch and tried to think of something interesting to occupy her time in the coming days or weeks—but without knowing how long they'd be there, it was pretty much impossible to come up with any really involved ideas. No point in spending time looking for a job or trying to make friends when their stay was only temporary. And if she did, she'd have to find a sitter for Lara. She sighed. Maybe she could spend some time catching up with her friends on Facebook, and catching up on all the unread books on her Kindle while Lara napped.

Kyle called this the "hunting and gathering" stage of his investigation. He mostly spent his time talking to people, including doctors, hospital personnel, plus the state and local epidemiological experts. He wanted to gather all available information so he could then sit and study it, looking for patterns and possible pathological mechanisms. Depending what he found, he'd then design some study to confirm or refute his theory.

So for now, he was typically out all day, and when he arrived home, he still had to organize his findings and email his team. Despite living in the same space, Gretchen and Lara didn't get to spend much time with him these days. She shrugged and put her feet up on the coffee table. All in all, it was still better than if they'd stayed back in D.C. Violence in D.C. was getting so bad, she probably wouldn't have had the nerve to leave that crappy little apartment at all.

She felt much safer here.

CHAPTER 10

An unpleasant feeling of déjà vu swept over Daphne Mercer as her sole lunchtime customer slapped his menu down on the lace-covered table, shot her a baleful glare, and folded his arms across his chest. Judging from his jeans and work shirt, he was one of the local ranchers, out to get some lunch on a work day.

She steeled herself for the encounter, plastered a smile on her face, and went over to his table.

"Is there something I can do for you?"

He pointed at the menu as if its very existence insulted him. "What kind of a joke is this?"

Daphne could feel her smile stiffen. "What do you mean, sir?"

"This isn't real food. Fake soy meat and flimsy vegetables. I want a steak. *That's* real food. Got a lot of fence posts to plant this afternoon, and I need a solid lunch."

"I'm sorry, sir. I have eggs. I could make you an omelet."

He looked her square in the eye. "You mean to tell me, you open a café in the middle of Sibley County—*farm country*—and you don't serve any sort of meat?"

"Well, no, I—"

"That's a real slap in the face to us producers, I'll tell ya that." He glanced around and shook his head. "Should've known with all this frilly stuff, you must be from the Cities. Carrie knew what to serve in this town, God rest her soul." He stood to leave. "Good luck to you." Then he stomped out and slammed the door.

Stunned by his abrupt exit, Daphne stood next to the

deserted table, glanced around her beautiful little café, then burst into tears. New businesses took time to establish. She understood that. But she'd hoped for a better reception than this. At first she'd thought it just was one of those things, where a small town doesn't readily embrace someone new—especially someone from the Cities. And that was probably part of it.

But mostly, the menu itself seemed to be the object of scorn. People would come in for breakfast and look at her funny when they asked for bacon and she explained she'd opened the café to cater to a healthier diet. She offered eggs and milk-based items, but that was as far into the animal protein spectrum as she intended to go.

It was even worse at lunch. At least at breakfast, they'd frown and order eggs. But at lunch they often wanted a pork chop, a little steak, or those chicken finger things. Nothing else on her menu remotely satisfied them, and they usually just thanked her and walked out. This guy wasn't the first one to complain, but he seemed downright hostile.

At least most of them were fairly polite about it, but polite didn't help her bottom line. Daphne shook her head and wiped away tears with the back of her hand. The town was full of animal-eaters. Hardly seemed worth it to keep the place open for lunch. One thing was for sure: she was not going to be offering real meat items. Not on her menu. Not ever. Even if she had to change towns.

Today, she didn't even feel like standing there, hoping a customer would walk through the door—and stay to actually order something. She'd felt really tired and run-down lately, despite her healthy diet and lifestyle. It wasn't like her, and she hoped it was just the stress from watching her dream of running a small-town café begin to circle the drain.

With an exhausted groan, she dried her eyes with some paper napkins and went back into the kitchen to shut down the grill and all the other appliances. Then she went to the front door, flipped the sign to CLOSED, locked up, and headed down the block to her little apartment.

She opened the door and stepped inside, panting a little and feeling as winded as if she'd walked several miles, though she exercised regularly and it had only been a block. A Midwest-flat block at that. She set down her purse and knelt on the floor as Agnes, her cat and faithful friend of sixteen years, strolled over and flopped down onto her back. At least Agnes was always happy to see her. She scratched behind the cat's ears for a few minutes, trying not to notice the gray mask that betrayed her age, then stood and went into the bathroom.

Midafternoon sunlight streamed through the little bathroom window, revealing an alarming sight. No thirty-year-old's face should look like that, especially one who chose her foods so carefully and took such good care of herself with exercise and yoga. Lines more apropos of a sixty-year-old seemed to have bloomed overnight. Daphne touched her skin. So rough, like it was dead or dying.

She released her long, straight, dark hair from the ponytail she kept it in while working in the café and ran her fingers through it. Was it more brittle, or was it her imagination? She looked closer in the mirror, and noticed a few gray hairs in front that she hadn't seen before.

Trembling, she pulled down her lower eyelids and scrutinized the tissue there. Pale, as if she were anemic, even though she was very careful to supplement her diet with iron and B vitamins.

She flexed her hands. Over the past few weeks, she'd noticed stiffness in her joints, as well as vague, random pains in her muscles. She'd chalked it up to all the scrubbing and physical labor needed to renovate the café. But the symptoms had lasted longer than they should have, considering when she'd completed that work. Cooking—what little she'd been called upon to do—and running a cash register should not cause these sorts of symptoms.

Turning away from the disturbing image in the mirror, she hurried to the living room, grabbed her laptop from the coffee table and turned it on. A search showed only a few doctors in the area. She expanded the search to include the Twin Cities. She'd be more likely to find somebody good closer to the Cities.

Something felt wrong, and she didn't want to fool around with some country quack trying to figure out what it might be. It'd be worth the drive back to the Cities to get the problem resolved quickly.

CHAPTER 11

"*I know* you don't want to be here, but we need to get you some new shoes and I need to get some things for dinner before your dad gets home from work."

Louise Dahl held eight-year-old Kennie by the hand and half-towed him through the doors of the Le Center Walmart. The kid hated to go shopping on a normal day, but for some reason, today he'd pitched a fit like no other before she could get him out of the house and into the car.

Maybe it was genetic. She didn't really want to be here, either. She hated shopping in general, hated the cavernous Walmart in particular, and wasn't entirely comfortable with their corporate policies. But it was where she could afford to shop, so there was just no getting around it. And Kennie's feet no longer fit in his damned shoes. This shopping trip could be put off no longer.

She steered him inside, where the octogenarian greeter pushed a cart toward them, smiled, and said, "Welcome to Walmart" in the tones of an automaton. What a shitty job, but maybe it was all he could get. Age discrimination likely kept him from anything more rewarding, poor guy. Louise smiled, nodded, and accepted the cart.

As they passed the greeter, Kennie pointed back at him. "Is that *all* he does all day?"

Louise gave him a small tug. "It's not polite to point. Yes, I think that *is* all he does all day." She glanced back toward the greeter, grateful to see that he hadn't noticed Kennie's pointing, or at least he didn't *appear* to have noticed. Kennie was just being a frank eight-year-old without filters, but she knew his comment would sting, had it been heard.

She released his hand so she could steer the cart. "All right, you stay close to me. The more cooperative you are, the sooner we can get out of here and go home, okay?" Sounded like a good bargain to her.

"Okay, Mom." Kennie didn't sound convinced, but at least he was cooperating for the moment.

Louise spotted the children's shoe section and turned the cart in that direction. And then Kennie stopped moving.

"Do we *have* to?"

Louise stopped the cart and crouched down to look Kennie in the eyes. "Yes, we have to. You know you've outgrown your shoes and they hurt your feet. We'll get some a little bigger that fit, okay? The shoes are just over there. I promise you, we'll get out of here as quick as we can, but you *need* a new pair of shoes."

Kennie looked unconvinced. He stared at the floor. "I don't wanna."

Louise stood and let out an exasperated sigh. "C'mon, I don't want to argue with you here."

Several loud bangs in quick succession cut off their budding argument. Screams erupted from the front of the store. Louise grabbed Kennie and held him close. She didn't know which way to go, or if there was a way out other than how they'd come in.

More shots rang out, cutting off a couple of voices mid-scream. "Oh God, oh shit …" Muttering and trembling, Louise dragged Kennie behind a nearby clothes rack and pushed him to the floor. For once, he cooperated and didn't argue with her. She crouched over him and peered out from below the bottom of the clothes.

From their hiding place, she could only see shoes and lower legs. People were running down the main aisle, screaming and crying as they went. She shuddered. What the hell was going on?

"Mommy, I'm scared …"

"Quiet."

She pulled out her cell phone and called 911 with one hand while she kept her other hand clapped over Kennie's mouth. The two rings before someone picked up seemed an eternity. She didn't know how long she'd be able to talk, so the words rushed right out when 911 picked up.

"Hello? I'm in the Le Center Walmart. Someone's in here shooting. I don't know how many are hurt. Some for sure, but I can't see from where I am. Send help quick. Okay, thanks."

She slipped the phone back into her purse and took a deep breath. More shots and screams. Kennie pulled away and let out a panicked wail. She clapped her hand back over his mouth and hoped he hadn't been heard over the rest of the chaos around them.

The gunshots stopped, so Louise peered beneath the clothes again to see if they had a chance to escape now. She tightened her grip on Kennie when she saw the solitary pair of black work boots walk slowly down the aisle, then stop. The boots turned in her direction and she held her breath, hoping whoever it was couldn't see them huddled on the floor behind the clothes rack. She closed her eyes tight, as if that would help.

Something slammed into her, throwing both her and Kennie backward. For a split second, she didn't understand what it was, then the loud bang and the pain registered in her brain. Her T-shirt clung to her, sticky, warm and wet. Gasping, she pressed a hand to her wounded shoulder, then checked Kennie.

He lay face-up on the floor, pale and fighting for breath, his lips tinged with blue and his eyes glassy. The bullet must have gone through her and hit him. She pressed her hand to his neck to try to stem the terrible flow of blood that had already formed a pool around him.

Louise breathed in jagged, hitched breaths. Her entire world seemed suspended in a haze of pain and confusion. Was he still there, waiting to finish them off? How could she get help? She felt light-headed, like she was going to pass out any minute. Then who would take care of Kennie? She had to stay conscious somehow. Somehow.

She heard another loud bang and a scream that died out all too quickly. He must have moved on. She dared a peek beneath the clothes again. No boots. Stay or go, stay or go? She heard more screaming, a male voice shouting, and what sounded like a scuffle. Then sirens. She kept her hand pressed to Kennie's neck and wept. Thank God for sirens.

CHAPTER 12

"*Tonight's top local story: a twenty-two-year-old resident of Gaylord was arrested late this afternoon after an incident at the Walmart in Le Center. Witnesses report that he entered the store, and when the greeter said hello, he pulled out a semiautomatic weapon, screamed something nonsensical laced with expletives, and opened fire. The greeter was killed instantly, and eight other people inside the store were injured before he was tackled and subdued.*" The young female news anchor paused a moment, as if trying to collect herself, and then continued. "*Some of the injured included small children. No names have been released at this time, pending notification of the next of kin.*"

The camera moved to the male co-anchor, who looked almost as distressed as his partner. "*In related news, the Sibley and Le Seuer county jails have become overcrowded to the point where fights have broken out among the prisoners, resulting in numerous injuries and one death so far. The danger both to the prisoners and to jail personnel has become so great that, in an unprecedented move, the county sheriffs have agreed to move most of the recent violent offenders to the Lakeside State Hospital, the mental health facility in western Sibley County, while they await the normal trial process. The ACLU has already announced they will be filing an action to oppose the move on numerous grounds. Back to you, Kelley.*"

Her face showing obvious relief at being able to switch to a less horrifying topic, Kelley switched gears entirely and began to report on the anticipated crop yields.

Gretchen clicked off the TV and tossed aside the remote. "Oh my God! I almost took Lara there today to get her some clothes. Good thing she's in bed and didn't see this story. For God's sake, this kind of stuff just doesn't happen in little towns like this. Sure, the occasional one-off murder or drunken spree, but not this widespread, large-scale violence—almost for the sake of violence itself."

Kyle reached over and held her tight, grateful to have her safe by his side. "I'm so glad you weren't there today. That's way too close to home."

He set his jaw. As if he wasn't already painfully aware how critical his assignment was, the news story threw a few asterisks and exclamation points on the matter. The jails in these little towns never filled up. Never. And certainly not with people so intent on killing or maiming anyone they could get their hands on. He shook his head. And Gretchen and Lara could easily have been there today, in the wrong place at the wrong time. He didn't even want to think about that.

He stood and began to pace. "I just have to work harder and faster to find out what's causing this. Something is. I just know it."

Gretchen looked up at him. "I wish I could do something to help."

Kyle stopped and glanced toward his work area, then back to Gretchen, and then back again as if he had to do something, but couldn't decide what. "I know, but I can't think of anything you can do to help. I just have to do the work to figure this out." He paused, then stared off into the distance as he thought aloud. "I wonder if I can take advantage of having all the violent offenders housed in one place with diagnostic equipment."

Alarmed, Gretchen sat forward on the couch. "Are you serious? Those people are dangerous."

He leaned down and kissed her. "I'll be careful. I promise. You know, it is really important to me that you and Lara are here—even if it seems like I'm ignoring you both right now. I don't mean to. I just have to get on top of this thing, no matter what it takes."

Kyle went to his workstation, sat, and opened up his laptop. "Whatever it is, it has to be identified and stopped. And fast."

CHAPTER 13

"You can sit up now, Daphne." Dr. Lucy Sloane began typing notes into the computer on the exam room counter. "When we get done here, I'll send in the nurse to do the blood draw. I'd like to run a complete panel to start with, especially since you're a new patient and we have no baseline labs in your records."

"All right." Daphne sat up and rubbed her arms to try to warm herself. The paper gown was no match for the exam room's chill.

Dr. Sloane cocked her head and scowled at the computer screen. "Looks like there's a typo in the file. It says you're thirty. How old are you?" She held her hands poised over the keyboard, ready to correct her records.

"What do you mean?" A hollow feeling of dread crept into Daphne's stomach. "I *am* thirty."

Dr. Sloane shot her a shocked look. "I … I'm sorry, but your skin, your muscle tone. It's more like that of a fifty-year-old."

She approached Daphne, peering at her closely as if examining her for the first time. "We already discussed your vegetarian diet. You've been supplementing with soy protein substitutes and taking vitamins to cover your B-complex and iron requirements. All the right things." Her voice trailed off with a puzzled tone.

Daphne began trembling. It was never good when a doctor looked at you like you were a freak, like something never seen before. She'd hoped whatever her problem was would have some simple explanation, some simple resolution. This just wasn't right. She took good care of herself and refused to eat the crap most people called food.

Dr. Sloane stepped back and rubbed her chin for a moment. "Well, let's start with the blood work and see what it shows. I'll have them put a rush on it. Meanwhile, I'll do some research. I haven't seen anything like this, and may have to call in a specialist to assist. But let's take it one step at a time, okay?"

"Sure." Half-formed questions swirled through Daphne's mind. But judging from what the doctor just said, there was no point in asking them now anyway. She gazed off into the distance, so distracted she hardly noticed when the doctor left and the nurse arrived to draw her blood.

"Make a tight fist for me, okay?"

"Huh? Oh." Daphne closed her eyes and made a fist as she tried to guess what the doctor really thought about her symptoms.

"I *said*, you can relax now. You're all done."

Daphne snapped open her eyes. "What? I'm sorry, I—"

The nurse picked up her plastic carrier of blood-drawing supplies and smiled. "It's all right. We'll get your sample in to the lab right away. You're in good hands with Dr. Sloane. She's a great diagnostician. Have a good rest of your day." She gave a brief nod and closed the door behind her as she left.

Daphne glanced down at the cotton ball taped to the inside of her elbow. Needles normally freaked her out. Dr. Sloane's reaction had upset her so much she hadn't even noticed the blood draw.

Daphne gazed out at the farm fields as she drove back home from the Cities in her Prius. On her left stood a field of corn, already about halfway grown; on her right, the lush green of soybean plants extended as far as the eye could see, bathed in warm afternoon sunlight. She still couldn't believe that such beautiful land could exist so close to a major metropolitan center like Minneapolis–St. Paul. The deep late-July green of the fields and crops helped to take her mind off her problems, at least for the moment.

She opened her window and drew in a deep breath of the humid midsummer air. The earthy smell and feel of it helped to ground her and chase the chill of the doctor's exam room from her bones and her soul. She felt a little better, but still couldn't shake the feeling that something was wrong with her. Something very wrong indeed.

CHAPTER 14

"*Of course* I realize what I'm asking is outside of normal protocol." Kyle ran a hand through his hair as he paced in the office of Dr. Fred McKinsey, the Minnesota state epidemiologist. Despite the brisk air conditioning, Kyle could feel sweat trickling at his temples and beneath his arms.

His status as an EIS investigator had made it easy for him to get an appointment with Dr. McKinsey. State epidemiologists normally worked with EIS to solve tough epidemiological mysteries. But now he was asking for something that—no matter how necessary he thought it was—could bring all manner of heat and bad press down on the state office. Old gray-haired McKinsey likely had his reputation to think about, and so was having none of it.

"Look here, those people are inmates awaiting trial—not research subjects at our disposal." Dr. McKinsey shook his head. "Civil rights organizations won't stand for it. The public—"

Kyle stopped pacing and glared at McKinsey. "With all due respect, sir, that's where I think you're wrong. The public would support just about anything right now. This violence has become an epidemic in every sense of the word. Big city, small town—doesn't matter. It's everywhere, and it's malignant."

His face red, McKinsey slammed his hands down on his desk and stood. He jabbed a finger in Kyle's direction. "Medical ethics are *not* controlled by public outcry. You went to a fine medical school. You should know that."

Kyle approached McKinsey so they faced each other eye-to-eye across the desk. He spoke in a low, urgent voice. "I do. And I agree with you—under normal circumstances. But this isn't normal. Don't you have statewide plans for protocol in the event of a biological outbreak?"

He placed his hands on McKinsey's desk and leaned forward, desperate to press his point. "Don't tell me if an outbreak of MERS or Ebola suddenly erupted, that you wouldn't activate quarantine and isolation protocols. That's a pretty serious curtailment of individual rights, wouldn't you say? But under some circumstances, it's justified, right?"

His face still deep red, McKinsey pursed his lips and sat back down. "Yes. We do. If we had some contagion at play here, I—"

"But that's my point! There *could* be contagion at work here. It's spreading too fast for any other explanation. Unless we conduct an organized study on those who are almost certainly suffering from whatever this is, we miss any hope of finding the root cause and stopping this."

McKinsey took off his glasses and rubbed his eyes. "What are you suggesting, then? How invasive?"

Kyle stepped away from the desk and chose his words carefully to exploit the opening. "I agree we'd have to proceed with great care, and not overstep where it can be avoided. I'd like to start with functional MRIs to see if there is some brain activity abnormality they all share in common. No dyes, no radiation. Noninvasive."

McKinsey put his glasses back on, drew a deep breath, and drummed his fingers on his desk for several moments before answering. "All right. I'll give the order under emergency protocol. I hope the fMRIs will provide some useful results that can help us narrow the search."

"Thank you. I really appreciate it." Kyle stepped forward and extended his hand. He tried not to show how relieved and surprised he was that he'd managed to talk McKinsey into the tests.

Now he just had to hope that the fMRIs hit pay dirt, because right now, he had no good working theories at all—only a gut feeling that there was some underlying cause at work that he had to discover and defuse. Before it was too late.

CHAPTER 15

Kyle pulled his rented Camry into a parking spot at their hotel. He killed the engine, then rested his arms and forehead on the steering wheel while he breathed deeply and tried to regroup. The drive back from St. Paul had been a nightmare. A semi had jackknifed on southbound I-35, the main north-south artery. The resulting multi-mile traffic jam, combined with his tense encounter with Dr. McKinsey, had exhausted him. As much as he loved little Lara, he hoped they could get her to bed early without a scene. No way could he handle her boisterous enthusiasm tonight.

After a few minutes, he sat up, rubbed his eyes, and flexed his tired shoulders. Then he grabbed the messenger bag containing his laptop and papers, locked the car, and took the elevator to their second-floor suite.

"It's Daddy! Woot!" Lara came charging out of the kitchen at full speed with her arms held out. She skidded on the entryway linoleum and collided with his leg before he could avoid the impact.

"Ow!" Sharp pain shot through his shin. He set his bag on the floor and crouched down to rub his leg.

Unfazed, Lara turned and started trying to open his bag with her inquisitive three-year-old hands.

"Let go of that!" Kyle snatched the bag away before she could get into it and mess with anything.

Lara flopped down onto the floor. Her face turned beet-red and tears began to flow as she howled in surprise and frustration.

"What is going on out here?" Gretchen came out of the

kitchen, frowning and drying her hands on a dish towel. "Why did you yell at Lara?" She took one look at the crying tot and rushed toward her.

Kyle barely restrained a groan. He'd only just walked in the door, tired as hell, and the scene had broken down into chaos, tears, and dirty looks from Gretchen. Just what he needed after the day he'd had. "She was about to get at my computer and papers—"

"Well, why'd you put them where she could get at them? You're the adult here." Gretchen sat on the floor, cradling Lara, who stared up at him with wide, innocent, tear-filled eyes.

"Because she'd just smashed into my shin, and it fucking hurt, okay?" He scooped up the bag, stomped over to his work desk, and set it down with a dramatic flourish. "There. Safe."

"Watch your language! I'm sure she didn't mean to do it."

Kyle whirled around. "I *know* she didn't mean to, all right? I've just had a very difficult day and I'm tired. I walk in the door and *bang*, she nails me. I'm sorry, I'm just not up for much of anything. I think I'll just go to bed now."

"But we haven't even had dinner."

"I'm too tired to even eat. You go ahead."

Kyle left Gretchen sitting on the floor with Lara crying anew, went into their bedroom, slammed the door, and prepared for bed. He stared at himself in the mirror as he brushed his teeth. Lara didn't deserve to be snapped at like that. Neither did Gretchen. But for God's sake, he didn't deserve to come home after a day like this and be hit with drama from the both of them.

The pressure to find the answer to the epidemic weighed on him more each day. He needed breathing room to find that answer before more people died. Maybe he should have come out here by himself after all. Then he would have had no distractions to get in his way.

"You awake?"

Kyle flinched as he awoke to the words. "Now I am."

"Sorry. I just wanted to talk about what happened tonight." He stole a glance at the nightstand clock's green digits.

Midnight. Terrific. He turned toward Gretchen in the dark and hoped he could keep the discussion brief so he could get back to sleep. "I'm sorry. I shouldn't have been so short with her. Probably should have called from the road and let you know how tired I was. Could have avoided the whole thing if I'd given you a heads-up."

"What happened? Bad traffic?"

Kyle sighed. "That was part of it. Big tie-up on 35, couple lanes shut. Drive back from St. Paul took at least double what it should have. The other thing was my meeting with the state epidemiology chief."

"What was so bad about that? I thought you were just going to give him a summary of your findings so far."

Kyle gave a short, caustic laugh. "If only it were that simple. Gretchen, I *have* no findings. I've been working on this thing for weeks and all I've got to show for it is a lot of lists. No pattern yet. I just *know* there's something going on—but I have no clue what. So instead, I pretty much demanded that he authorize something that I would never ask for under normal circumstances."

"What?" Gretchen sat up in the dark.

"I asked him to order functional MRIs for all those inmates being held at Lakeside State Hospital. I wanted to see if there's a pattern in their brain activity."

Gretchen gasped. "You mentioned that the other night, but I didn't think you were serious. Do you really have the power to ask that?"

"I have the power to work with local epidemiologists to design studies to resolve epidemics. I know this treads into dangerous territory. These people are not patients, and they're not going to be asked for their consent. At least fMRIs are considered physically noninvasive."

"I take it this was a hard sell."

"That's an understatement. It was a very difficult conversation. I don't think we have any other choice, but I still don't feel good about doing this."

"Are you sure there's no other way? Can't you minimize the problem by asking for releases?"

"No time. I don't know how long it's going to take to track down the cause—let alone the solution. We're already behind the eight ball. Too many people are being killed or maimed every day." He shook his head. "I can't do the same thing Dad did."

"What's that?"

"Dad didn't retire early from practicing medicine for the usual reasons. He did it because he felt so guilty about a particular case, he couldn't bring himself to practice another single day."

"What happened?"

Kyle sat up, drew his knees to his chest, and bowed his head. "That depends on who you ask. The patient's family sued for malpractice after she died, but all the experts said Dad did everything appropriate to try to diagnose the problem. It was genuinely elusive. But that's not how he saw it. When the autopsy revealed the cause of death, he became convinced he should have figured it out in time to save her. If he'd worked just a little smarter, harder, or whatever. If he'd run that one last test. If, if, if. Well, it ruined him. He no longer trusted himself as a diagnostician and he eventually took that belief to his grave. I'd just been accepted into med school when this happened, and it hit me hard. I promised myself I would not go through all the work, training, and sacrifice to become a doctor and then allow something like that to happen. So, I have to find out what's behind this problem, and time is not on my side."

Gretchen put her hand on his shoulder. "I know you've been harder on yourself with every passing day. But you're not being reasonable. We've been here less than a month. You're doing everything possible."

Kyle lay back down and rolled over, facing away from Gretchen. "Dad thought he was doing everything possible, too—until it was too late. I can't let that happen. I have to find the answer, no matter what it takes. Too much is at stake."

CHAPTER 16

Pinkish foam oozed from the cow's nose as she lay on her side in the straw. Marty Janssen leaned against the side of the wooden stall in the dimly lit barn. He'd brought her inside to care for her, but nothing he tried seemed to work. He knelt beside her and pressed his finger to the carotid artery beneath her jaw.

Nothing.

Another one gone.

Marty stood, wiped his hands on his jeans, and sighed. Fourth one just this week. One—maybe even two—he could chalk up as a fluke. Shit happens on a farm. The animals aren't pets and he wasn't attached like that. But something wasn't right. And his bottom line wouldn't put up with it for very long, either.

All the cows that had died this way were young, but they'd just lost their will to live and gone down fast as if they'd been years older than they were. He ticked through the possibilities in his head. They'd all had their vaccinations. Unless the vaccines were defective, it shouldn't have been any of those diseases. They'd all had antibiotic mixed in their feed. He didn't care for that practice, but the bigger corporate farms did it to keep up yields, and he had to follow suit to stay in business. Nope, shouldn't have been an infection. Not bacterial, anyway.

Marty was fresh out of ideas. He used the best soy-based feed on the market, premixed with antibiotics and vitamin supplements. His herd had been thriving on it for years now. The feed mix cost more up front, but it more than paid for itself in enhanced yields.

He shook his head and pulled his cell from his pocket. He

had the vet, Les Anderson, on his speed dial. You never know when there's a breech delivery and minutes count. Don't want to go fumbling for the damned vet's number. He punched it.

"Les here."

"Yeah, Doc, it's Marty. Got a problem."

"What's that?"

"Another cow dead. Fourth this week. All the same symptoms. I've tried everything, but they just go downhill and die on me. Need you to come out here and take a look. Can't have this keep happening."

"Sure thing, Marty. I'll try to get out there later today. Like to take some tissue samples from the one that just died."

"Thanks. See you later." Marty ended the call and slipped the phone back into his pocket. He stared down at the dead cow. He'd never seen anything like this in all his years of farming. He sure hoped Doc would be able to figure it out before it ruined him. Last year had been tough enough with the drought. His yields had been terrible and he hadn't broken even on the year. He'd hoped this year would be better.

But it wasn't looking very good right now.

CHAPTER 17

"Here's a hard copy of the results. I'll send it to you soft as well." Dr. McKinsey handed Kyle a half-inch-thick, bound report, then seated himself at his desk.

"Thanks." Kyle started to flip through the report. "Have you had a chance to look at this yet?"

Dr. McKinsey folded his hands on his desk, leaned back, and avoided eye contact. "Yes, I have. The results are remarkable and incontrovertible—as far as they go."

"How so?" Kyle closed the report and watched McKinsey's body language to gauge his degree of buy-in for the inmate testing.

He shook his head in amazement. "The areas of the brain associated with aggression lit up like a Christmas tree in the fMRI of every single subject tested."

Kyle let out a low whistle. "But why?"

"That's the problem. The fMRI tells us the *what*, but not the *why*. You'll see when you look at the images in the report, the results were so absolutely consistent, you'd think they were multiple studies of the same brain. That makes me believe that we're looking at a unified cause here, but what it is, I have no idea—at least not from just this study."

McKinsey's response suggested he'd be amenable to taking the testing a step further. Kyle decided to exploit the opportunity. There was no time to lose, and the fMRI results screamed for follow-up despite the ethical complications. He cleared his throat and forced the words from his dry mouth with what he hoped was a confident, casual tone.

"Dr. McKinsey, you know we're going to have to track down

the *why*." He waved the report in the air. "You said yourself these results are suggestive of a common root cause. We can't stop now."

McKinsey folded his arms across his chest and scowled for a moment before answering. "Understood. What do you propose?"

Spurred by McKinsey's receptivity, Kyle sprang out of his chair and paced, counting off the ideas on his fingers as they came to him.

"More extensive studies focusing on organic factors that influence brain function. I want to see full blood chemistries, including assays for all neurochemicals associated with aggression and stress. Check blood pressures—maybe there's a pattern there. And gut bacteria cultures. There've been some important studies lately showing that different species of gut bacteria affect brain function via neurochemical influences."

He stopped pacing and faced McKinsey. "None of these tests may yield the answer. They may only lead us a level deeper. But I think these are the most appropriate studies to perform next, and they're still relatively noninvasive."

McKinsey sighed, took off his glasses, and rubbed his eyes. "I agree with your approach in theory, but that's a lot of lab work—both in terms of processing volume and expense. And I barely managed to get the fMRIs ordered. Got a lot of pushback on that because of resources and cost."

Kyle sat back down and leaned forward in his chair. "If you can arrange for the sample collections, our labs can handle the processing and analysis. We have the staff and budget for it back at the CDC, so that's no problem. The fMRI results clearly point to something unusual going on. You should be able to use that to counter any resistance. It's the only way we're going to have a hope of getting this figured out and under control. The violence has done anything but abate. Public safety is at stake—additional tests are justified."

McKinsey held up his hands, palms toward Kyle. "I agree with you, but I'm in a position where I have to do a little selling first." He stood. "I'll take care of it. Might take some wrangling, but I'll make sure it gets done as soon as possible."

Kyle took his cue, stood, and shook hands. "Thank you. Let me know when to expect the samples to arrive at our lab."

CHAPTER 18

Daphne stabbed the bookmark into her paperback novel and slammed it down on the counter. She glanced around her café at the—once again—nonexistent lunch crowd. She felt like crap as it was, and to drag herself in to wait for customers who never came only made things worse.

To add to her foul mood, Dr. Sloane had called earlier with her lab results. Inconclusive. The values were normal. Well, normal for a person about twenty years older than she was. She wanted her to come in for some additional, unspecified tests to try to pin things down.

She loathed the idea of undergoing more tests while the doctor went on a diagnostic hunting expedition. For that matter, she hated needing a doctor to intervene in her health at all. A healthy diet and lifestyle should be all you needed, absent something like a broken leg.

But what if they *did* figure it out, and it was something serious?

Daphne decided to close up shop for the day. She doubted she'd miss any stray customers in her absence. Once outside, she pocketed the café key and watched heat ripples rise up from the sidewalk amid the stifling midsummer heat and humidity. She chuckled for a moment at the contrast. In Minnesota, you endured intense heat in the summer. And then in the winter, you could experience cold so profound your lungs wanted to freeze if you took too deep and sudden a breath.

Despite the sweltering heat, she decided to take a little stroll along the main street before heading back to her apartment. She'd been so tired lately, she's fallen out of her exercise routine, so it might do her some good to get some outdoor air. It was, after all, one of those glorious days in the Upper Midwest when the deep blue sky itself appeared limitless, the billowy white clouds as if they were miles higher than clouds anywhere else.

Daphne walked slowly, taking the time to glance inside the windows of the shops and businesses along the way. They all looked like they were from another time, when things were simpler. She liked that. It was why she'd come to this town.

The hair shop offered men's and women's cuts. No frills, just the practical stuff. One station for nails, for those so inclined. The town bookkeeper operated out of a little storefront with a wide window bearing his name in script. You could look in and see his receptionist sitting there behind her desk. A small-town bank, housed in an older brick building with intricate stained glass in the windows.

Daphne wiped her forehead with the back of her hand. Even the minimal exertion of her walk had started her sweating in the humidity. She felt a little dizzy, and decided she'd best head back to her place, drink some water, and make sure the AC was going strong.

Trembling, she made her way back the block or so to her apartment and stepped inside, grateful to escape the heat. She dropped her purse beside the door and bent down to pet Agnes. The old black cat slunk over and greeted her by weaving around her ankles, yowling, and blinking her green eyes.

"Hey, there. Glad *someone's* happy to see me."

She picked her up and hugged her close to her chest. She and Agnes had been together for years, and the vibration from her loud and steady purring always soothed Daphne when she was upset. She went into the kitchen to get a glass of water, then, exhausted, collapsed onto the couch to watch some television. She was too tired to care what she watched, so she just left it on the news channel and cuddled Agnes.

"Widespread reports are coming in of foods that are spoiling far earlier than their sell-by dates. The problem affects meats and animal products: beef, pork, and poultry, fresh as well as cold cuts and other prepared items. It's also affecting milk, cheese, yogurt, cottage cheese, and other milk-based products. Eggs have been

affected, too, as well as all products made with eggs, like cakes and other baked goods.

"The foods appear fine in the store, and have good sell-by dates when purchased. But they spoil quickly, even with proper refrigeration. No explanations have arisen so far, and the problem is not limited to a single supplier."

Daphne smirked. Her diet was safer and healthier than a diet that included animal-based products. Just more proof.

CHAPTER 19

"Thank you." Kyle accepted the steaming cup of coffee from Gretchen without taking his eyes off his laptop screen. He had a full day ahead of him, and with any luck, maybe some answers at last.

"So what's going on now?"

"The lab results from the CDC just arrived in my email. I really need to concentrate right now."

She sighed. "All right. Maybe I'll get Lara and take her outside to play."

He turned to face her. "I'd really appreciate it if you would. This is a massive report, and I can't afford to miss anything, no matter how subtle. I've got to dig through it quickly and thoroughly."

Gretchen tried to peer over his shoulder at the laptop's screen. "It's all right. I understand, really I do. It's just that sometimes I feel … well, I wish I could help out somehow. You're pouring all your energy into this, and I don't have all that much to do except take care of Lara. Guess I should maybe check out the town more."

"Maybe you should. Just be careful out there. Look out for anyone behaving strangely."

"I will. I'm still really on guard after that Walmart incident." She kissed his cheek and nodded toward his laptop. "Hope you find what you're looking for in there."

"Thanks."

Relieved to be left alone to work in peace, Kyle opened the enormous PDF file and began scrolling through its contents. Fortunately, the CDC lab had aggregated the results, so not only did the report contain individual results by subject number, but for each specific test, there was a graph or chart depicting the pattern of results across all the test subjects. That would make his work at least somewhat easier.

He started with the summary-level charts. Blood cell counts, liver and kidney chemical studies—all within normal ranges. The rest of the blood chemistry charts also appeared disappointingly normal. Anxious to find something out of the ordinary, he turned to the hormone level studies.

In every subject—male and female alike—the testosterone level was within normal range. He took a sip of his coffee, sat back, and stretched his shoulders. That made no sense in light of the fMRI studies. Activity in the amygdala had been striking in every single case, and elevated testosterone was known to cause activity in that part of the brain. He'd expected to see high testosterone levels.

Why would people with normal testosterone levels uniformly show brain activity consistent with sky-high levels? Given the widespread violence throughout the nation and beyond, in urban and rural settings alike, he could not believe the cause was a local environmental issue. It couldn't be.

He scrolled through page after page of graphs, each relentlessly showing normal distributions of results. Something had to be in there, somewhere. He just had to find it. He chugged the rest of his now-cold coffee, then hunched forward as if peering at the screen more closely would force the report to reveal the gem he needed.

At last he spotted something abnormal—and quite odd. Each subject's test results showed exceptionally low levels of serotonin. He frowned and considered this development. Serotonin acted as an antagonist to testosterone. Could their serotonin levels be so low that even normal testosterone levels caused abnormal levels of aggression and brain activity in the amygdala?

Kyle scoured all the remaining blood work results and found nothing else outside normal limits. Next was the section containing the gut bacteria analyses. Gut bacteria could produce mood- and personality-altering neurochemicals that traveled to the brain via the vagus nerve. Maybe he'd find something useful there.

As the day wore on, he waded through pages and pages of individual test results, then came upon a single page that summarized and compared the occurrence of various species of gut bacteria both in the test subjects and in the general population. He rubbed his burning eyes and tried to refocus them on his laptop screen. Grateful to see the information presented in aggregate form, he carefully studied the long list of bacteria.

And then he saw it. There was one species—and one species only—that was common to every test subject. *Bacteroides metasonis. B. metasonis* occurred naturally in maybe forty-seven percent of the general population. But here it was in every single test subject. Statistically impossible. There had to be a connection.

Kyle quickly emailed his contact at the CDC lab to culture the *B. metasonis* ASAP, determine what chemicals it emitted, and to test it on lab mice to see if introducing it into their guts resulted in aggressive behavior.

He leaned back in his chair, closed his weary eyes, and rubbed his aching neck. He had to be on the trail of this thing at last. Those findings were too consistent to be a statistical aberration. Without exception, each subject had brain activity consistent with aggression, ultra-low serotonin levels, and hosted a particular, not overly common, gut bacteria. It had to be significant.

But what was the mechanism, the trigger? Without that piece of the puzzle, even this much progress was still for naught. He'd already been on the case a month, with nothing actionable to show for it. And the violence had not only increased throughout the nation, but had also begun to spread to other countries while he was stationed out in Farmtown, USA, searching for the needle in the haystack.

He opened his eyes, leaned forward and stared at his laptop screen. He'd just have to work harder, that's all. No distractions. Nothing else mattered until he nailed this thing. He would not let what happened to Dad happen to him.

CHAPTER 20

Gretchen felt transported back in time when she pulled into the little town of St. Joe. She'd seen about all there was of Gaylord where they were staying, and so she'd decided to drive the short distance to where Kyle had been focusing his investigation after that horrific murder.

She parked her rented Camry at the curb and stared out at the scene. She half expected characters in costumes like those from the *Twilight Zone*'s "A Stop at Willoughby" episode to stroll across the little grassy park in the center square, but the place was pretty much deserted. Maybe people were afraid to be out these days. Who could blame them after that Walmart incident the next town over? She'd certainly begun thinking twice before venturing out these days.

"Where are we, Mommy?" piped Lara from her car seat in back.

Gretchen twisted in her seat to answer. "St. Joe. Cute little town, huh?" She found it hard to imagine such a grisly murder could have occurred here. The town square looked downright idyllic in the early August sunshine.

"I'm hungry!"

"Me, too. Let's find a place to eat."

Gretchen absently rubbed her growing belly. The humid summer heat still bothered her, but at least she'd finally gotten past the morning sickness and her appetite was back in full force. A little lunch would be good about now.

She locked the car after extracting Lara from her car seat. Funny, it looked like the kind of place where you wouldn't need to lock up, but in light of everything that had been going on, there was no sense taking chances. She took Lara's hand and they started off down the block.

"It's hot!" Lara squirmed and acted like she had somewhere else to go where it would be cooler.

"Hang on a minute. I see a café right on the corner there. I'm sure it's air-conditioned inside."

"Ohhh … kay." Lara did not sound convinced.

Moments later, they stood in front of the café. It looked the very image of small-town, with its picture window, *Daphne's Café* painted onto the glass in flowing lavender script, and pretty little white-and-lavender-striped canvas awnings shading the front.

Gretchen opened the door and they stepped inside. A gust of cool air greeted them, much to her relief. She glanced around. The place was decorated as cute as can be with healthy green indoor plants all over the place, but … there wasn't a single customer in there. She glanced at her watch. Lunchtime. While she wasn't one who liked crowds, she took it as a bad sign that what appeared to be the only café in town was utterly devoid of customers right when it should be bustling.

A tired-looking older woman slumped behind the counter. She straightened up when they entered, smiled, and motioned with her arm. "Please, sit anywhere you'd like."

Gretchen selected a table right by the main window. The town looked quiet, but if any trouble erupted, she'd want to know about it so she could—could *what*, exactly? She wasn't sure of the answer to that, but it still seemed best to position herself to keep an eye on things.

She sat Lara in the chair next to her so she could help her eat. She still had a toddler's tendency to play with her food if she lost interest. Gretchen didn't want her flinging something and making a mess in the tidy little café.

"Hi, I'm Daphne." The woman handed Gretchen a menu.

"So you're the owner?" Gretchen motioned toward the writing on the window.

"I am. Been here a little more than a month." Daphne smiled, but then the smile faded.

"Well, congratulations. You have a pretty little place here."

Daphne glanced around, her smile disappearing entirely. "Yeah, thank you. I worked hard to make it like this."

Gretchen began to feel uncomfortable. There was a story here, and she wasn't sure what it was. She sensed that all was not good in Daphne's world for some reason. She glanced at the menu and her face must have registered surprise.

"Is there a problem?"

"No, I … well, Lara usually likes chicken nuggets when we go out. They're sort of a treat for her."

"We have vegetarian options available. Soy chicken nuggets. Would that work?"

Gretchen again glanced at the menu, unable to believe what she was seeing. Given that this was beef country, she'd been in the mood for a really good, messy cheeseburger, but could see that wasn't going to happen. Not at this café, anyway. "Yeah, that'll be fine. I'll have, well, I guess I'll have the grilled Portobello mushroom. We'll both have water."

"Thank you." Daphne took the menu and disappeared into the kitchen.

"What's soy?"

"Don't worry about it. It'll taste like chicken." Gretchen decided not to try to explain to Lara that it was better for her than fried chunks of ground-up dark meat. That piece of information would ensure Lara would hate it. She stared out the window and tried to muster up some enthusiasm for a big grilled mushroom.

No wonder there were no other customers.

Gretchen pushed aside her empty plate. Daphne was a whiz with herbs and seasonings. *Unbelievable a mushroom could have so much flavor.* Maybe it was better sometimes to try things with an open mind. She glanced at Lara's plate. She'd nearly finished her soy chicken nuggets, despite a rocky start when she bit into the first one and declared that it did not, in fact, taste like chicken.

Daphne came by with the check. "So, was everything okay?"

"Yes, very good. But I have to say I was surprised there was no beef or chicken on the menu—especially in a town like this."

Daphne lowered her eyes. "Yeah, you and everyone else. At least you stayed and gave it a try. You must not be from here."

"No, we're staying in Gaylord for a while. My husband is with a branch of the CDC. He's out here working on an investigation. It just strikes me that this is a pretty meat-oriented area, and to have a vegetarian menu, well, it might make it a little tough on business."

"Oh, it has. I'm from the Cities. Got tired of the way things had gotten up there and decided I wanted to have a small business of my own out in a more rural area. Thought a little café would be just the thing. But I've been vegetarian for a long time now, and I believe that meat and animal products are just not healthy for people to eat. So I didn't want to offer menu items I didn't think were healthy, that I wouldn't eat." She shrugged. "Besides, even if I didn't feel that strongly, I just don't know how to prepare those kinds of foods. I *do* know how to come up with vegetarian recipes that are good. Or at least I think so."

"I have to agree with you there. My lunch was delicious." Gretchen smiled. "I really didn't think it would be."

"Well, there you are. Too bad no one else around here has such an open mind. I get a little business for breakfast, since I do serve eggs and cheese. But lunch has been dead." She shook her head. "Though my breakfast offerings may change soon. It's been hard to keep eggs and cheese. They spoil so fast anymore, no matter what I do. Can't afford the waste. But if I don't offer at least those items with breakfast, I'll probably lose my morning customers, too."

She took a step back and waved her hand. "I'm sorry. I didn't mean to burden you with all that. You have a nice day. Thanks for coming by." She sniffed as if fighting off tears, slipped the check onto the table, and hurried back into the kitchen.

Taken aback by the entire exchange, Gretchen glanced at the check, then paid, leaving a generous tip. The older woman's story saddened her. She hoped her business picked up, but she suspected that was a pipe dream. Serving vegetarian food in the heart of livestock territory was likely more than a matter of taste—it was almost an insult to her intended customers.

"Come on, Lara. Let's head back home and see how Daddy's doing."

"Okay, Mommy. Can we have hot dogs tonight?"

CHAPTER 21

Ally James was running late. Again. Nothing pissed her off more, but it wasn't her fault. Really. It was those idiots who'd blocked up the main drag through town with their careless fender-bender. And that's what had put her behind. Not that she forgot the time and slung her purse on and flew out the door right about when the twins, Tina and Trisha, were due to be let out of class their first day in second grade. She could've made up that time if that accident hadn't screwed up traffic.

So now she raced her Honda Odyssey along traffic-free side streets like some character in a video game. She glanced at the dash clock. A minute before school let out. So she wasn't late. Not yet.

Ally glanced up and saw the Stop sign a hair too late. She mashed down the brake, sending the minivan into antilock-brake vibration mode—a mode with which she was not unfamiliar. The vehicle came to a stop several feet into the intersection. Fortunately, no one had been coming. She looked both ways and stomped on the gas pedal.

As she turned the corner a block or so from the school, she stole another glance at the dash clock. Two minutes late now. *Damn!* The school was in a good neighborhood, and there would be plenty of teachers and other parents around, but she still didn't like to have the twins running around unsupervised. Not with the way things had gotten, with all those crazy incidents. Bad things could happen to little kids—or anyone—in an instant these days.

Ally drew up in front of the school, but from this direction, she had to make a left to enter the pick-up circle. She flipped on the turn signal and braked to wait for oncoming traffic to clear.

She felt a twinge in her temples. An unpleasant one, like the beginnings of a migraine. Just what she needed. Tina and Trisha would be all excited with the events of their day and would be talking nonstop in those shrill seven-year-old-girl voices. The kind that could enter your ear and pierce your brain just like a searing ice pick before you could defend yourself. Enough to make your head explode under normal circumstances, but pure death when you had a migraine cooking.

The twinge worsened … and traveled. It became a presence, seeming to expand to occupy the entire inside of her skull. Ally pressed her hands to the sides of her head, as if she could force it back down into whatever hell it had erupted from. But no dice. If anything, it was gathering strength. She couldn't just sit here in traffic like this.

She took a quick look behind her, then jammed on the gas and cut across to the right lane. She made a right at the end of the block, then three more lefts, so she could position herself to eventually make a right directly into the pick-up area. She had to get the kids and get home so she could take something and lie down.

As she neared the school, an overflow of cars trying to get into the pick-up area clogged the entry and formed a line along the curb. She braked, took her place at the back of that line, and tried to calm down. For some reason that seemed to go beyond her burgeoning headache, she felt an urgent need for motion.

As Ally crept closer to the pick-up area—seemingly an inch at a time—she felt a strange sensation travel beneath her skin, sort of electric. It started in her hands and feet, tingling, then worked its way up her limbs and toward her trunk. She could feel her heart pounding and racing inside her chest as if she'd just run a few laps. Her head throbbed, and her muscles tensed as if she were bracing herself for something. She became aware of how hard she was clenching her teeth and tried to loosen her jaw.

Now she was wedged between cars, with others joining the line behind her. She felt trapped, frantic. What the hell was going on? She was usually full-tilt Type A, but this was different, and it was starting to scare her. Maybe she was having some kind of panic attack. She took slow, deep inhalations, letting the breath out slowly as she'd learned in yoga class.

Finally, some of the cars cleared and she reached the entrance to the pick-up area. She glanced at the sidewalk as she turned into the drive. Too damned many people milling around. Teachers, kids still waiting to be picked up, helicopter parents who couldn't just pull up to the curb and let the kids into the cars, but had to park and go walk the damned kids to the car. Suddenly, they all no longer looked human to her. They were just all moving *things*, cluttering the sidewalk with their presence.

Ally opened her mouth wide and let out a scream of pure rage. She didn't know where it had come from, and she didn't care. She gripped the wheel in both white-knuckled hands and clamped her jaw shut so hard and fast that several teeth shattered.

She spat out the tooth fragments, then slammed the gas pedal to the floor and aimed for the crowd. She wanted to clear them away, like the offending clutter they were. The minivan jumped the curb and cut down everything in its path. Bodies—adult and child alike—flew up and smashed into the windshield. The safety glass shattered into a sheet of what soon resembled red stained glass.

Ally couldn't see out the windshield anymore, had no idea which way she was going or whether she had succeeded in clearing everyone out of her way. She pushed the gas pedal down, gunning the engine mercilessly as a skull-splitting surge of pain and rage consumed her, first blocking out the screams, then the sound of crumpled metal as the minivan plowed into the brick schoolhouse.

CHAPTER 22

Les Anderson stood, then took his time wiping the sweat from his forehead with the back of his arm. He kept his eyes cast down toward the four dead cows surrounding him in the pasture, as if by avoiding eye contact, he could somehow avoid having to come up with a diagnosis—though of course he knew better.

He simply had no diagnosis to give. Despite all his years in practice and how much he prided himself on his diagnostic skills, he was flummoxed like never before.

Just last week he'd been out at Marty Janssen's place, looking at a dead cow that should not have been dead. Now, Paul Gorsham had called him out to take a look at several of his cows that he'd found dead this morning. No warning, no apparent illness, no injuries. Just dead. Looked pretty much like that cow of Paul's he'd examined some weeks back. Even though he'd taken blood and tissue samples after she died, the lab results had been less than illuminating.

He had a couple of calls scheduled at other farms later in the afternoon. Judging by the messages those farmers had left, he was in for more of the same—and it was affecting pork and poultry as well. He wished to God he had a clue what this was.

"So, what is it, Doc?"

Les raised his eyes and saw Paul standing by the nearest carcass, nervously fingering the baseball cap he held in his knobby, arthritic hands and looking at him with an expression both expectant and filled with dread. And right he was to be worried. Whatever was killing his cattle could kill his entire livelihood. The actual losses were bad enough, but the potential implications were even worse. If the cause of death—whatever it was—was found to be contagious to other livestock or a danger to human consumption in any way, he and many others like him would be ruined.

And he could just as easily be ruined by hysteria. Les well remembered the Mad Cow scare. But it had been limited to cattle and mostly a problem in the UK—at least as far as the American public knew. If there were even the hint of something similar spreading domestically, all bets were off on how much panic would ensue. Even if the problem couldn't possibly affect humans, the mere specter of Mad Cow or something like it would be enough to set off a chain of events that would ruin not just Paul Gorsham, but all livestock production.

"Paul, I really don't know what to tell you. Saw something similar at Marty's place, ran some tests, but couldn't find anything definitive—just like with that first cow you had die a few weeks back. I hate to say it, but I'm stumped."

"Well, you've gotta do *something*. Last year, with the drought … I'm on the edge already, Doc. If this keeps up, Susan and I'll lose the farm for sure." He glanced away as if fighting off tears.

"I know. Everyone around here's in the same boat, except maybe the BigAg spreads. Paul, if I'm going to get to the bottom of this, I'll need some help. I have a friend at the vet school up at the U. I'd like to take some new samples and send them to him. Unofficially, of course. He can be trusted to keep quiet unless there is something that absolutely has to be reported."

Paul scowled. "God, I hope this doesn't need to involve the authorities—or any sort of press." He stared down at the dead cow by his feet. "Do what you need to do." He put his hat back on and turned to head back to the barn.

Les had been in practice long enough to have a bad feeling in the pit of his stomach over this. He hoped he was wrong, but he usually wasn't.

CHAPTER 23

"Gretchen, will you *please* keep Lara in the other room and get her to be quiet? I need to focus on this call."

Kyle tuned out her response, adjusted his earpiece and fidgeted while he waited for the call to start. The monotonous on-hold music grated on him. Its endless looping mirrored his feeling that something important lay just beyond his reach while he ran in helpless, desperate circles.

Vic Rayburn had scheduled the conference call with all the EIS team members assigned to investigate the violence epidemic. Kyle opened his laptop and clenched his jaw as he again scrolled through the PDF file of the latest lab results. So close and yet so far. He understood the main mechanism now, but until he identified the underlying trigger, nothing could be done. Just like having emergency responders ready and waiting, but being unable to dial 911.

The obnoxious music stopped and Vic came on the line. "Thank you all for joining the call this morning. Let's get started. Kyle, I believe you're the only one with a new development. Tell the group what you've found so far in St. Joe."

Kyle cleared his throat. "Hi, everybody. I'll start with a brief rundown of what's been happening. It's pretty small-town out here, so it wasn't long before the local jails filled up with people arrested for various violent acts, up to and including murder. The overcrowding and the violence got out of hand, so they moved those inmates to Lakeside State Hospital while they make their way through the courts. We've conducted some tests on these individuals—"

"This is Jeff Franklin. I'm stationed in Los Angeles. How

did you get permission to test those people? I can't believe they allowed it."

"It wasn't easy, but I got the Minnesota State Epidemiologist to use his emergency powers to allow noninvasive testing on the inmates."

"Amazing. Out here, the jails are way overcrowded, but they just keep packing them in, despite all the violent incidents. No way will they let us run tests on the inmates. Maybe you actually got lucky they moved them to a mental institution."

"Maybe so. At any rate, we've run a number of studies so far that have yielded important information. We started with functional MRIs, which showed absolutely consistent results. Each person tested showed markedly elevated activity in the brain's aggression center, the amygdala. So we ran blood tests and sampled gut bacteria to try to find out why. I expected elevated testosterone levels given what the fMRIs showed, but testosterone levels were all normal. However, serotonin levels were extremely low in all the test subjects—so low that even a normal testosterone level would be sufficient to cause the brain activity we observed."

"But what would cause the serotonin levels to be so low?" asked Vic.

"That's where the gut bacteria analysis comes in. Each of the persons tested harbors significant levels of *Bacteroides metasonis*, a species of gut bacteria that only occurs in forty-seven percent of the general population—a statistically impossible result. I had the CDC labs culture the bacteria and test it in mice. Sure enough, the mice became aggressive when the bacteria were introduced into their guts. Turns out these particular bacteria produce a chemical that inhibits the body's production of serotonin, though *metasonis* isn't known to produce such a chemical."

"This is already a rather complex chain of causation, yet it sounds like there's still at least one other mechanism involved," said Vic.

"That's right. Something—we don't yet know what—causes *B. metasonis* to produce the chemical, serotonin is inhibited, testosterone is left without an antagonist, and so the aggression centers of the brain become overstimulated in the population that harbors this strain of gut bacteria."

Vic cut in. "Excellent work, Kyle. Did you also have the lab test whether the aggression ceased when the *metasonis* was eliminated with a suitable antibiotic?"

"I did, and the aggression did *not* cease. It appears once the brain changes occur, they are permanent. It is still possible that eliminating *metasonis* with antibiotic therapy *before* it's triggered into emitting the serotonin-inhibiting chemical could be a preventive measure. But normally this is a beneficial gut bacteria in humans. I don't know that we want to consider antibiotic therapy without knowing what triggers it to function in this particular way. Not unless we had no other choice."

"Good point. There's also the danger of creating a drug-resistant strain with widespread—and potentially scattershot—antibiotic use. I trust everyone has reviewed the file containing Kyle's results that I sent out ahead of the meeting. So, does anyone have ideas about the underlying trigger? I'm thinking it has to be something ingested—what else could influence gut bacteria?"

Kyle's shoulders slumped as he listened to the ensuing discussion drone on. It *had* to be something that all those affected had ingested, but his mind boggled at trying to narrow it down. Humans ingested all manner of food and drink. The problem had become so widespread that, whatever it was, it had to be something common. How in hell was he going to track this down? He felt a psychosomatic twinge in his stomach as he considered the nearly endless possibilities.

CHAPTER 24

Gretchen finished putting away the dinner dishes and went into the living room. And there was Kyle at his desk, hunched over his laptop and oblivious to the rest of the world. As usual. She walked over and gently put her hands on his shoulders.

"Come on. Lara's in bed; the dishes are done. You've been at it all day. Can't we just relax on the couch for a while? You need a break and I'd like to remember what it's like to have a quiet evening together." She rubbed her belly. "Especially before we're joined by Baby Number Two here."

Kyle spoke without even turning to face her. His tone was distant, almost as if he were talking to himself. "I've got to solve this. The longer it takes, the more it spreads. More people killing and dying while I sit here struggling. I think—I hope to God—I'm one answer away from figuring it all out. The trigger. What is the trigger—"

Gretchen gently shook his shoulder. "Kyle, you've been sitting in that same position all day. You even ate your dinner there. Sometimes it helps to step away for a while and let it percolate in the back of your mind. Works for me."

He turned and glared at her with bloodshot eyes, then spoke through clenched teeth. "It doesn't matter what works for you. It matters what works for *me*. *I'm* the one responsible for figuring this out." He slammed his fist down on the desk, scattering papers to the floor.

Gretchen stepped back, alarmed to see a side of her husband she didn't know existed. "Shhhh—don't wake Lara! You're losing perspective, Kyle. There's a whole team working on this, not just you. You are *not* the sole person responsible. Take a break before you drive yourself right into the ground."

He glared at her in silence for several moments, breathing loudly. Then he lowered his head and clapped his hands to his face. "Oh my God. I'm so sorry, Gretchen. You didn't deserve that."

She went over and put her arms around him. "It's all right. You're just overworking yourself. It's the stress talking."

"You're probably right. I've been staring at this all day, thinking of nothing else. It's starting to get to me." He sighed, stood, then followed her to the couch. "I'm really sorry. I shouldn't have talked to you that way."

Hoping to ease the tension, Gretchen tucked her legs beneath her and reached for the remote. "Forget it. Let's try to enjoy the evening for a while. Anything you're interested in watching?"

He slumped down onto the couch and waved his hand. "No, let's just relax. I'm sick of the news and I'm not up for a movie."

She turned to look him in the eye and wondered how much longer he could drive himself as he had been. He looked so drained and she felt helpless to lighten his load. "I understand what you're up against—and the stakes. Really I do." She stretched and smiled. "It's nice to have your undivided attention for a while, though."

Kyle smiled a little, kissed her, and held her close. "Tell me, what have you been up to these days?"

Gretchen nestled against him, relieved to see his mood lighten. "Well, Lara and I ventured over to St. Joe the other day, just for something new to see. Cute town. Hard to imagine what happened there, with that farmer killing his wife like that."

"Yeah, it's your stereotypical small farm town—except for the uptick in violence. That murder was the worst incident over there, at least so far."

"Well, I hope it doesn't get any worse. Anyway, Lara and I were hungry, so we stopped at a café on the main square. Adorable little place, but I'm not sure how long it'll last."

"Every small town like that has its main street café. I haven't had time to try this one myself. What's the problem with it?"

"Well, it's kind of odd. We met the owner. You can tell she

wants to make a go of it, really wants to do a good job. But she's hamstrung herself if she expects to succeed in this neck of the woods."

"How so?"

Gretchen laughed. "You won't believe this. She has a vegetarian menu. Imagine that, here in farm country." She shook her head. "She said business is bad. Well, yeah. Talk about not doing your market research before starting a business. She seemed awfully nice, though. But firm on her beliefs about animal products. She only goes so far as to serve milk products and eggs. That's it."

"That's just nuts. One look around would tell you this would be the least likely haven for vegetarians."

"I think she's finding that out the hard way. Funny, she touts it as healthier, but she didn't look all that healthy to me."

Kyle perked up. "What do you mean?"

"I don't know. Just didn't look healthy, or like she took good care of herself. Maybe she was just older. Hard to tell." She shrugged. "I feel sorry for her. Somehow I doubt she's going to last. Not in this town."

CHAPTER 25

Kyle started the Camry and snapped the AC to max. He'd just wrapped up an obligatory meeting with Sherry Nelson, the county's public health director, to bring her up to speed on what he'd learned so far. The meeting accomplished nothing concrete; it only served to keep him away from his work and ratchet up his nerves. He had to find the last piece of the puzzle. Nothing else mattered. Time spent on *anything* else only cost more lives.

The oppressive mid-August heat and humidity further fueled his dark mood. The brief walk from the county office building to the car had already plastered his hair down with sweat. He wiped the dampness from his forehead with the back of his hand as he waited for the AC to do its job.

After several minutes, the inside of the car became reasonably comfortable, a haven from the brutal steaminess outside. Kyle felt a little calmer as he let the cool air wash over him, then realized he was hungry for lunch. Gretchen's description of the vegetarian café piqued his curiosity, so he started away from the curb and drove the short distance to St. Joe.

As he pulled into town, he spotted Daphne's Café on the main drag. It looked flat-out lonely. Though it was lunchtime, he had his pick of parking places right in front. Gretchen was right. No one was around. The café, as well as the town center, was dead.

He went inside and glanced around. Not only was the café a vegetarian island in the middle of beef and farm country, it was also a little too … sweet. Too much pastel and lace. Fluffy, frilly décor likely wasn't a great draw to those in a hardworking farm town like St. Joe.

A tall, thin woman came out from the kitchen area and stood behind the counter. She looked genuinely surprised to see him. "May I help you?"

"Yes, I'd like to have lunch."

She swept her arm to indicate the entire place. "Sit wherever you'd like. You have it to yourself. Menus are on the tables."

Her tone carried a bitter edge, and her appearance and bearing were that of an older woman. Kyle tried to get a better look from where he stood without being too obvious. She did not look well to him. Something about her skin—the texture and the pallor. Maybe it was the stress of her business doing so poorly; maybe it was something more.

Kyle took a seat at one of the tables by the window and turned his attention to the menu. While he wasn't a huge meat eater, the menu didn't particularly appeal to him. It was hot out, though, and he was in the mood for something lighter anyway.

The woman approached his table after a couple of minutes. "Have you decided?"

"Yes, I'd like the marinated garbanzo salad, and water."

"Okay. Be right back."

He watched as she went back into the kitchen. Her gait indicated some sort of stiffness or pain in her hips and low back, possibly her knees as well. He wondered why someone her age would try to start a business like this, where she'd have to stand for long periods—at least, she would if she had any decent volume of business.

She returned with his order moments later, set the plate and glass down on the table, then stood with her hands on her hips. "Anything else?"

His curiosity getting the better of him, Kyle gestured to the empty chair across the table. "Why don't you have a seat? I wouldn't mind a little company while I eat. I'm a visitor in town."

She raised one eyebrow and shrugged slightly. "Sure." She lowered herself into the chair with a degree of care that usually indicated widespread joint pain, then offered her hand. "Name's Daphne Mercer. Why would you be visiting here, though? It's not exactly a tourist stop." She gave a slight smile.

"My name's Kyle Sommers. I'm a doctor in a special CDC program. I'm out here on assignment to find out if there's an epidemiological basis for the surge in violence."

She tilted her head. "Oh? I think I may have met your wife the other day. She had a cute little girl with her. Unless there's more than one of you assigned out here."

"No, just me. There are others in other locations. Yes, that was my wife Gretchen and our daughter Lara."

Daphne smiled briefly, then turned serious. "So, you think it's a virus or something?"

"I wouldn't rule that out, but right now we're thinking it's a more complicated process involving something people are ingesting. In certain cases, there's an interaction with intestinal flora in a way that causes neurological changes associated with extreme violence."

She gave him an I-told-you-so smirk. "I've always been a big believer that you are what you eat. People are so indiscriminate about what they put in their mouths." She slumped forward. "But I guess I'm in the minority in thinking that way—or else you wouldn't be the only customer in the place."

"Why do you say that?"

"Well, the menu, of course. Vegetarian. Seems I picked the wrong place to try to serve healthy food."

"I take it you're a vegetarian, then."

"Sure am. Been that way most of my thirty years." Kyle nearly choked on a garbanzo bean. No way did this woman look thirty. Maybe she wasn't properly supplementing her diet. "Are you strictly vegan?"

"Yes. I take supplements to get my B-complex and iron, and I eat a lot of those soy substitutes, like soy chicken, soy burgers, things like that, to make sure I get complete protein. I do serve eggs and dairy products on the breakfast menu, though." She shook her head. "But I may have to stop doing that. The stuff goes bad so fast. The sell-by dates are worthless these days. And it's so gross, like the protein starts to … *disintegrate*. If I moved the stuff a little quicker, it might be okay, but I don't."

Something clicked in the back of Kyle's mind. There had been news stories on the sell-by date problem, not just for eggs and dairy, but for all animal products and meats. Gretchen had taken to shopping for only small amounts of those items at a time so they could eat them before they went bad. Why was that happening? Could it have anything to do with his investigation?

"—I think I'll be lucky to last a few more months."

Kyle realized she'd been talking while he'd been caught up in his train of thought. "I'm sorry, what were you saying?"

She frowned. "I was saying, if things don't change, I don't think I'm going to last much longer here."

"I'm really sorry to hear that." Kyle suddenly wanted to get back to work, to follow his train of thought to see if it took him anywhere useful. He glanced at his watch. "I'm sorry, I just realized I need to get going."

"Sure, I'll get your check. Thanks for coming by." She gave him a tired smile, rose stiffly from her chair, and returned to the counter to ring up his order.

Kyle watched her, wondering what made her look so much older than her actual age. She seemed to be supplementing her diet properly. Could be anything, he supposed. Maybe she had some chronic condition.

Right now, he had a feeling he might have a lead—and he needed to make the most of it.

CHAPTER 26

Dr. Lucy Sloane stood by the exam room counter and peered at her computer screen as if willing it to reveal a secret to her. At last she straightened and faced Daphne with a puzzled frown on her face.

"I've never seen anything like this before. Your initial lab results were normal—for a fifty-year-old. This newer set also reads normal—for a seventy-year-old, and it's only been a few weeks since we ran the first tests." She folded her arms. "I really don't know what else to do but to refer you out to Mayo. If there's any place that has seen something like this, it would have to be them."

Daphne wanted to reject Dr. Sloane's words as if they had physical presence. She wanted to snatch them, hurl them across the room, watch them crash into the wall and break apart. This couldn't be happening. Not to her.

But she couldn't deny the lab results, no matter how strange they were. She'd known something wasn't right, or she wouldn't have gone to the doctor in the first place. And she'd only felt worse and worse in the ensuing weeks, mirroring the decline in her labs. Something was going on in her body, and it was serious. She could tell that much. But what? Dr. Sloane was an experienced, well-respected doctor in the Twin Cities. If she was baffled enough to throw in the towel and refer her to Mayo, it had to be a tough case.

"Daphne, I think you should get an appointment scheduled as soon as possible. Whatever is going on, it's clearly progressing quite quickly. If there's a way to stop it, you need to find out right away … while there is still time."

If there's a way to stop it … oh, that's just great. Daphne raised her hands, palms out. "I'm sure you're right. I just can't think about it right now. I feel completely overwhelmed."

Dr. Sloane moved closer and placed her hand on Daphne's shoulder. She leaned down, looked into her eyes, and spoke gently. "Would you like me to make the arrangements for you? I can do that if it would help. In fact, I can probably get you in a little faster if I make that initial contact for you. May I?"

Daphne trembled, feeling vulnerable in her paper exam gown, her bare legs hanging off the side of the exam table. She stared down, allowing her eyes to follow the patterns in the faux wood flooring while she mustered the courage to even look at Dr. Sloane, let alone answer her.

"Daphne? Can I get you some water?"

She looked up to see Dr. Sloane staring at her with a concerned look on her face. She knew she had to get to the bottom of this, but was terrified of what she'd find.

She spoke in a whisper. "All right. Go ahead and call Mayo for me. My schedule is flexible."

Daphne lingered in her Prius, not yet ready to face much of anything, let alone the outside world. She'd closed her eyes and rested her forehead on the steering wheel while she tried to pull herself together enough even to begin the drive home. For the moment, she was grateful for the cocoon-like feeling inside in her car in the dim light of the parking garage.

She'd felt a heavy sense of foreboding after her first visit with Dr. Sloane, but she'd been able to cloak it in denial until today's visit. Now she felt like she was being pushed down a path that could lead nowhere good. Mayo would either also be baffled, leaving her in the same hellish limbo—or they would find the problem. Daphne had a feeling the answer would not be a happy one. Her body seemed to have aged forty years in a matter of weeks. Even if Mayo figured it out, how could the damage be reversed?

She sat up and examined her hands. The skin was leathery, alligator-wrinkled. She'd even developed those brown spots you see on older women who'd sunbathed indiscriminately in their youth. She glanced in the rearview mirror. Age lines traversed her face as if she'd suddenly turned into her grandmother. She shifted in her car seat. Her back, shoulder joints, hip joints—all were stiff and painful.

And every day it got worse. As if she were disintegrating, as if her structure had begun to crumble. She wondered how much worse it would get, and what other frightening developments she had yet to face.

CHAPTER 27

Kyle pulled up to the hand-carved wooden sign at the end of the driveway that read LES ANDERSON, VETERINARIAN. Early morning light played across the sign, emphasizing the age and grain of the wood. The place was on the outskirts of St. Joe proper, and comprised what appeared to be a combination house/veterinary clinic, as well as a barn and corral, probably for those animals needing the farm animal equivalent of hospitalization. It looked like an efficient, well-designed setup.

Dr. Anderson agreed to meet him there at 6 a.m., before he began his morning treatments and house-call rounds for the day. He'd said once he got started on those things, his day's schedule could spiral right out of control, depending what presented itself. So first thing would be the best.

Kyle was fine with that. The earlier the better. He was anxious to see if his hunch would yield the answer he needed. He went up to the front door and pressed the buzzer.

Moments later, the door opened and an older man with a face that appeared both kindly and no-nonsense stood before him. "Hi, I'm Doc Anderson. Just call me Les. You must be—"

"Kyle." He smiled and extended his hand to shake.

"Come on in. Let's talk in my office." Les led him into a room just to the right of the front door containing a desk stacked high with papers and texts, a small couch strewn with magazines, two aqua vinyl guest chairs that looked like originals from the '50s, and walls of shelves jammed with books.

Kyle took a seat and only then noticed that a computer did in fact lurk on the desk behind a particularly tall stack of papers. He'd briefly wondered how anyone could practice medicine of any sort without the Internet in this day and age.

"So, how can I help you?" Les leaned back in his chair and steepled his fingers.

Kyle explained how he came to be in St. Joe and what he'd learned so far. "So now I'm trying to find out what causes *B. metasonis* to emit the chemical that suppresses serotonin production. It's got to be something people are ingesting, but what? I'm wondering if there's a connection with these reports of animal-product-related foods spoiling before their sell-by dates. Why are they going bad so quickly? I figured since you work with livestock, maybe you've seen something or have some ideas."

Les leaned forward, rested his forearms on the desk, and clasped his hands together. "Funny you should say that. I don't do slaughterhouse or production inspections, so I can't speak to the sell-by problem. But I have been seeing some disturbing things lately."

He rifled through a stack of papers until he found what he was looking for. "I've been getting reports of cattle, pigs, and poultry dying before their time. Now, these animals have been vaccinated; they've had proper supplements in their feed. No signs of obvious disease. Yet the animals are dying. The best way I can describe it is that they appear to be dying of premature old age. Very premature."

An image of the café's owner appeared in Kyle's mind. *Premature decay.* He leaned forward in his chair, eager to hear more. "Why?"

"Well, it was stumping me—and of course, the farmers were upset. The last thing they need is something killing their animals now, after last year's drought. So I looked through all my texts, looked all over the Internet. Nothing. Finally, I took some samples and sent them off to a friend at the vet school up in the Cities. I wanted to keep it informal for the time being. No need to cause a panic."

"I see. And what did your friend say?"

"That's the hell of it. I just heard back from him. He did find something—and it's consistent. He found it in beef, poultry, and pork tissue samples. He also spotted it in egg and milk samples."

"What was it?"

"In all the samples, one of the key amino acids in the protein—valine—is malformed. It's the mirror image of what it should be. Given the symptoms and manner of death I've seen in these animals, I'm thinking this malformed valine does something to destabilize proteins in the body's tissues and products, so the animals essentially age much faster than they should. That's my theory, anyway. I haven't told anyone else about it yet, because I wasn't sure what to do next."

Kyle could barely sit still in his chair. "That could explain the sell-by date problems, too, don't you think? Destabilized proteins in the various types of animal-based products. Now I have two more questions: why is the valine improperly formed in the first place, and when it's ingested by humans hosting *B. metasonis*, what happens? Is that what somehow triggers the bacteria to emit the serotonin-inhibiting chemical?"

Les blew out a long breath as he considered Kyle's questions. "Let's think this through. Your second question sounds straightforward to test."

"I agree. I can arrange for that to be tested in the CDC labs easily enough. What about the first question?"

"I can work on that one. My friend at the vet school can help. See, if it's dietary, it may be easy to trace."

"How so?"

"All the various types of livestock share something in common, whether on small private farms or BigAg operations. The primary feed is soy-based, supplemented with vitamins and antibiotics. If we have a problem with a component of animal protein, then it may well stem from a problem with the protein they're being fed. And that would be in the soy."

"Really? What about corn or hay?"

Les waved his hand. "Nah. Feed corn's all taken up in ethanol production these days. Too expensive to use for animal feed. Hay? The drought did in the crop last year. Even if it hadn't, the name of the game is quick development. So farmers use a GMO soy mix—usually with some growth hormones thrown in for good measure. Makes the livestock grow faster, so more money at the market. And GMO because GMO soy is all tricked out to grow faster and resist weeds in the first place, so the feed can be mass-produced cheaply. I can take care of testing the feed. What say I do that and you have your people test the flora's response to the screwed-up valine? I can get you a sample of that to work with."

"Sounds good." Kyle rose and extended his hand. "Thanks for taking the time, Les. I really appreciate it. We may be able to get to the bottom of two problems at once: your prematurely aging livestock and my crime wave."

"You're quite welcome. Thanks for stopping by."

Kyle got into his car and sped home, anxious to email new test requests to the CDC lab. There had to be a connection, he could *feel* it.

CHAPTER 28

Marty stuffed his leather work gloves into his pocket and ambled over to the fence. "Hey, Paul. What brings you here?"

"I heard back from Doc on some tests he ran."

Marty noticed that Paul looked about four shades too pale. "Which tests? What's the matter?" He hoped there wasn't some outbreak in the offing. His property adjoined Paul's and any contagion would likely visit him quick enough. As if he didn't have enough problems already.

"I had some cows that died. Doc said it looked like from old age, but they were young."

Marty's muscles tensed. "I've been having some of that, too. He took samples, but he told me the results were inconclusive."

"Yeah, he mentioned that to me. So this time he sent the samples out to some friend of his at the vet school up in the Cities, sort of on the QT. Results came back that one of the amino acids is twisted funny."

"Oh?"

Paul slouched his lanky shoulders and leaned on the fence as he dug the toe of his boot around in the dirt. "Well, he didn't know what to think at first, so he did more tests on some chickens and hogs that had the same problem. Same amino acid was wrong in all of them. He thinks it's what's causing them to age and die prematurely, because it screws up the protein structure in their muscles and other tissues."

"Well, how'd the amino acid get screwed up in the first place?"

"He's running more tests right now and said he'd let us all

know. He's thinking it's something in the feed."

Marty smacked his hand on the fence post. "Christ! In the *feed*? We all use pretty much the same feed!"

"That's why he's thinking it's something in the feed. It's affecting all different kinds of livestock, and it's affecting more than just you and me."

Marty took off his cap and vigorously scratched his head. "Well, what the hell are we supposed to do? Last year's hay crop failed. There's nothing else *to* feed but the soy mix. Are you saying we could be killing 'em with their own feed?"

"Could be. Let's see what Doc comes up with. Gotta head back. I have another downer cow waiting for me as it is." Grim-faced, Paul turned and headed back toward his property, his posture and gait weighed down with dread.

Marty felt like he'd been kicked in the gut by a mule. If Doc was right, he might as well take a flamethrower to his spread. There'd be no saving it.

CHAPTER 29

Kyle gulped the last of his morning coffee and glanced at the kitchen clock. Eight already. The CDC lab may have emailed him the test results, and that vet had undoubtedly been up for hours by now. Maybe today would be the day he'd get the answers he needed.

"Sorry. I need to get on the computer and see if anything's come in for me."

Gretchen set Lara down in her playpen and gave him a sour look. "Thanks, I'll just clean up the breakfast dishes and bathe Lara myself."

He barely bit back a cutting remark. What else did Gretchen have to do all day anyway? He had to solve this thing, *yesterday.* People were dying, and he'd be damned if he'd let what happened to Dad happen to him. He'd leave no stone unturned until he got to the bottom of this. Rather than waste even more time getting into an argument, he shrugged and strode out to his computer.

Kyle flung himself into his chair and opened his laptop. He tapped the screen to force the email to sync, to be sure he had the most recent communications in front of him. An email from the vet appeared. He opened it.

Kyle,

I had my friend test samples from the three most popular brands of soy-based feed. Each of them contains the malformed valine in the soy protein. I'm going to have him test a couple more brands for good measure, but I can tell you these three brands make up the bulk of the feed used in these parts. So now we know the source of the malformed valine. It's coming right from the GMO soy that's the main ingredient in these feeds. Livestock take it in and metabolize it to produce and replenish their own protein-based bodily components. And that's how it's getting into the animal protein products. What have you found out?

Les

Kyle hunched over his PC, every muscle taut. With only one question left to answer, he *had* to be on the brink of figuring out the root cause and entire mechanism of the violence epidemic. He tapped Refresh again. And again. He stood and paced, then tapped Refresh again. Then he picked up his cell and called his contact in the CDC lab.

"We were just finishing up the written report."

"Send it on when you can. Tell me now. How does *B. metasonis* respond to the malformed valine?"

"Pretty much as you'd suspected. Once exposed to the malformed valine, *B. metasonis* secretes the serotonin-inhibiting chemical—and it keeps on doing it, even when the faulty valine is removed from its environment. It's like it turns on some gate that can't be turned off. But, in fresh colonies of *metasonis* exposed only to normal valine, no serotonin-inhibiting chemical. The faulty valine is definitely the trigger—an irreversible trigger at that."

"Thank you." Kyle hung up the phone. He sat at his desk, trembling, as the full meaning of his discovery hit him. He had it now, the entire mechanism.

GMO soy had somehow developed a defective valine molecule, the mirror image of what it should be. This caused two related problems.

When ingested by livestock in *plant protein* form in commercial feed, the metabolized valine formed unstable tissue proteins, leading to premature deaths of the animals themselves, as well as the abnormally short shelf lives of animal-based products. And all animal-protein-based products—meat, dairy, eggs—from these livestock incorporated the defective valine.

In humans who harbored *B. metasonis* in their gut flora, the bad valine, when ingested in the form of these animal proteins, caused *metasonis* to secrete the serotonin-inhibiting chemical that triggered irreversible brain changes leading to extreme aggression.

Kyle sat back in his chair, breathing shallowly as the implications unfolded in his mind. The food chain was broken, perhaps irretrievably. And it had broken in a way that had created the worst wave of violent crime ever. How on earth could this be stopped?

Could it be stopped?

CHAPTER 30

Daphne glanced at her empty café and checked the time. Yet another nonexistent lunch rush. She'd only had a couple of customers come in for breakfast, and absolutely not another soul had stepped in the rest of the day. Except the mailman, but only to deliver her mail, look at her like she were a leper, and leave before anything could rub off on him. Her business and her dreams were dying a slow death right before her eyes.

Without thinking, she got off her stool a little too quickly. A searing pain spiked through her hip joint and down her leg, forcing her to grab hold of the counter to keep from falling. It had been getting worse every day. Pretty much the exact opposite of when she'd broken her foot some years back and, after the initial stages, could feel the pain lessen a notch each day until one day it was gone. She'd quit exercising entirely weeks ago and couldn't hold even the least demanding yoga postures anymore.

She gritted her teeth and limped to the front of the café, flipped the sign to CLOSED, and locked the door in the unlikely event someone bothered to come by. Time to face some reality. She went into her cramped office behind the kitchen, eased her pain-racked body down into her chair, and opened her business checkbook. The balance was pathetic. She glanced at the stack of unpaid bills that she kept in the top right drawer. Clearly a mismatch involved.

As she wondered how much longer she could go before falling behind on her bills, her cell rang. The caller ID showed the call was from Mayo. She hesitated, then took a deep breath and answered it.

"Ms. Mercer, this is Dr. Lowell Adams from Mayo."

"Yes?"

"We've received your lab results. Is this a good time to talk?"

"Sure." *Why not? Make my day.* For some reason, she didn't think it would be news worth celebrating.

"Ms. Mercer, the results are consistent with those your primary care provider reported to us from your previous tests. Normal blood chemistries, but for someone much older than you."

"Yeah." She closed her eyes and rubbed the bridge of her nose.

"We also received the results for the tissue sample we took. They were ... unusual."

Daphne rubbed at the spot on her thigh where they'd taken a punch biopsy of her muscle tissue. She'd forgotten about it until now, even though it hadn't been healing as quickly as it should. It was probably all in her head, but the site had just begun to throb.

"Unusual?" Daphne could feel something twitching in the pit of her stomach. *Unusual* is not the word you want to hear when the doctor calls with lab results.

"As I'm sure you know, protein is made up of amino acids, which in turn are assembled in a specific way from various molecules. In your muscle tissue, you have an unusual form of the amino acid valine. It's the mirror image of what it should be."

Daphne had trouble catching her breath. "So what does that mean?"

"I wish I could say for sure. We haven't seen anything like this before—I checked. But given how protein synthesis works, we're thinking it's causing you to age prematurely. When the faulty valine is metabolized in your body, the resulting tissue proteins lack structural integrity. We think this is why you're experiencing the symptoms you are."

"But what started this?"

"That's even more of a mystery right now. There's no way to be certain, but given how quickly your symptoms have progressed, this is likely not something that's been present all your life. So something has either triggered your system to manufacture the faulty valine, or you're ingesting something that is causing the valine to take this form."

Daphne put her hand to her face and bowed her head. She didn't know whether to scream or cry, but she didn't want to do either while she was still on the phone. "But I'm so careful about what I eat. I don't eat meat or animal products at all. I only eat fresh fruits and vegetables, with some soy products for protein and vitamin supplements for B-complex and iron."

"Tell me more. The fruits and vegetables. Where do you get them? Any pesticides?"

"No. Only organic, pesticide-free."

"What about the vitamins?"

"A known, national brand."

Dr. Adams paused. "What about the soy products?"

"Mostly the Second Nature line, those frozen ones. I like their texture the best."

"I'll want to check into those. I'm pretty sure they're made with GMO soy. Do you eat a lot of them?"

"Yeah, I do, actually. They're pretty good, and I figure the soy provides a complete protein in place of meat."

"It does, but right now I'm interested in anything that might explain how you've wound up with mirror-imaged valine molecules. Do you have any opened packages of it on hand?"

"Well, yes, I do."

"I could get some at the store, but I don't want to introduce any unknowns into the analysis. I'd like to run tests on samples you've actually eaten from, if I could. Can you bring your opened packages up to my office?"

"Yeah, I can do that."

"As soon as you can, please. I'd like to start testing as quickly as possible."

Daphne glanced at her watch. "I can still get up there today, if you like."

"That would be great. I'll alert the receptionist, so in case I'm with a patient, you won't need to wait."

"Thanks, bye." Daphne ended the call and set down her cell. She took a deep breath and let it out as she slumped over her desk. She felt like she'd just fallen right down a rabbit hole.

CHAPTER 31

Vic Rayburn shook his head as he scrolled through the latest Internet news stories on the violence epidemic. He hoped his team would get to the bottom of it soon. People were becoming afraid to go out, businesses were shutting down, the economy was in havoc, and the problem had spread to other countries now. Crackpots were advancing their latest theories all over the Internet, which only stoked the fear factor.

He was glad he didn't live far from his office. But summer would be over soon, and the shorter days of fall would take over. Vic didn't feel all that safe himself after dark anymore. He set aside his gloomy thoughts and answered his phone.

"Hello, Vic? It's Kyle. I've got it figured out, the whole thing."

He leaned his elbows on his desk and gave Kyle his undivided attention. No one else working on the problem had found more than a small possible link here or there. Nothing cohesive. "Fill me in."

Kyle told Vic what he'd learned about the defective valine in the soy-based feeds, what it was doing to livestock and livestock-based products, and how it worked to trigger *B. metasonis* to emit the serotonin-inhibiting chemical that caused all the other physical and behavioral changes. He explained his methodology and how he finally pieced it all together.

Vic pinched the bridge of his nose as he took in the information and tried to find flaws in Kyle's methods or conclusions. "But wait. The defective valine has a different effect in animals than in humans?"

"Yes. Apparently when it's ingested in plant protein form— as in the case of livestock consuming GMO soy-based feed—it results in defective tissue proteins that age prematurely, if you will. That applies to muscle and other bodily tissues as well as proteins produced by livestock, like milk, eggs, and cheese. But when it's ingested in the form of animal protein from these sources, it sets up that trigger effect in the forty-seven percent of the population who harbor *B. metasonis*, resulting in the violent behavior. But even in those who have *metasonis* in their gut, no animal protein, no violent changes."

"I see. Is this a problem only with soy that ends up in animal feed? What about soy products for human consumption?"

Kyle remained silent for a moment. "That's a good question. I don't know if this form of valine has appeared in those products. If it did, I'd expect a similar mechanism as I've found in livestock. But when livestock consume their feed, that's their only source of valine. A human would have to get all or most of his valine from soy products to experience the same effect. In such a case, I'd expect weakened protein structures, premature aging."

Vic's initial relief that the answer had at last been found quickly turned to growing alarm as he realized the full ramifications of what Kyle had told him. A terrible, terrible flaw had worked its way into the base of the food chain, and it had already led to an epidemic of unprecedented violence and an impending economic meltdown. He again struggled to find a flaw in Kyle's analysis, and could not. Of course he would double-check everything, just to be sure, before formally releasing the information to the public. "What do you think can be done about it, Kyle?"

"I'm afraid there may not be much that *can* be done. Once the defective valine triggers *metasonis* to produce the chemical, it's already too late. Once that switch is tripped, it stays tripped, and the effects on the brain are irreversible anyway. The only hope is that there may be some who harbor that bacteria who haven't yet consumed animal products containing the faulty valine for whatever reason. We might have a small window of opportunity there. Probably very small."

Vic ran a shaking hand through his hair. "My God."

"That subpopulation would have to be identified and treated with a suitable antibiotic to eliminate *metasonis* from their guts before the mechanism could be tripped. I don't know how the hell that could possibly be done in time, and I'm not sure such a subpopulation even exists at this point."

"We could analyze the trajectory of new cases of violence. If the frequency of new incidents starts to taper off, it may mean that all those who will be affected, have been."

"That makes sense. I suspect there's likely no treatable subpopulation left to chase anyway. Also, we'll need to get the USDA involved in this. Livestock deaths and problems with animal-based food products are their bailiwick, right?"

"Yes, but I'm sure they've never faced anything like this before." Vic tried to steady his trembling hands. Kyle was right. The food chain was devastatingly broken. The only saving grace was that it apparently wasn't a problem for those who didn't harbor the specific bacteria, at least at this point. That was something, anyway. "I'm not even sure how you restore food safety—let alone public confidence—in the face of something like this."

"I know. I've started trying to think that through, and it's huge. Just huge. Even if you destroy all the defective soy meal and all the products it's entered, you'd still have to ensure that any GMO soy crops going forward don't contain the faulty valine. And you'd have to reestablish new lines of all the affected livestock: beef and dairy cattle, sheep, poultry, pigs."

Vic took a deep breath as he tried to wrap his head around the magnitude of the problem. As difficult a job as finding the root cause had been, the search for the solution promised to be even worse. How do you tell the entire population that the food they eat had created a public health—*and* public safety—emergency of unprecedented scope?

"Excellent work, Kyle. I'll need your written report ASAP so we can conduct an accelerated peer review before releasing the information to the public and the other agencies that need to know about it."

Vic hung up the phone, then closed his eyes and put his head on his desk. In all his years with the EIS, his teams had unraveled some tough public health mysteries. But never anything this catastrophic.

CHAPTER 32

Marty Janssen pushed up from his crouched position and eased the painful kinks out of his knees and lower back. The paunch he'd developed after Ellen died didn't help matters. Weary, he leaned against the side of the stall and stared down. Another dead cow. Same thing. That premature aging problem. Doc had told him the same as he'd told Paul: something about the protein structure being wrong. The feed he'd been using had caused it. Just what the hell was he supposed to do? Hay hadn't even been an option this year. The soy-based feed, with its added vitamins and antibiotics, was the most cost-effective. But now, he'd learned, it was killing his animals.

He let out a long, exhausted sigh. He'd hoped to eke out a slim profit this year and stay afloat. Forget about that now. Soon he wouldn't have a herd left at the rate he was going. Doc didn't even know if there was any way to reverse the process and stop the losses. Marty didn't know what to do. Maybe he'd talk to Paul later and see what he was thinking.

He decided to dispose of the carcass tomorrow. It's not like the cow had died of anything contagious. He was just too worn out to bother right now. He left the barn and headed for the house, first stopping at Ellen's grave.

As he gazed down at the late-season wildflowers surrounding her tombstone, a sudden wave of sorrow struck him, almost like a solid mass of pain. Maybe the flowers triggered it, with their tired, wilted blooms drooping, signaling the end of the growing season, the shortening of days. Maybe it was all too much. He wished Ellen were still with him. She'd always been his strength. But at the same time, he knew it would break her heart to see what was happening to her beloved farm. He turned away, the sense of loss overwhelming him. First Ellen, now the farm.

Marty stepped into the mud room, kicked off his work boots, and washed his hands and face. Then he poured himself a nice tall slug of bourbon and went into the living room to catch the news before dinner. He plopped himself down on the couch and clicked the remote.

"… *for more on this breaking story, here is our science reporter, Ben Wheaton.*"

Marty smirked. The guy *looked* like a science nerd, with his slicked-down hair, thick glasses, and dead-serious expression.

"*Good evening. The CDC announced today that a special team has solved the mystery of the wave of violence that has been sweeping the world. It's a great piece of investigation with far-reaching implications.*"

Marty took another gulp of bourbon and turned up the volume.

"*They found that those exhibiting the violent behavior all harbor a certain species of gut bacteria, B. metasonis. We all have various species of intestinal bacteria in different combinations. They help digest our food, and they also can influence mood and behavior because of the chemicals they emit. In this case, they're emitting a chemical that suppresses serotonin, which normally regulates the effects of testosterone. So in those people affected, even normal levels of testosterone cause ultra-aggressive brain function patterns, and the change appears to be permanent once it happens.*"

Marty leaned forward. Could this be what happened to Dustin?

"*These particular bacteria emit that chemical only when they're exposed to a malformed version of valine, an amino acid present in animal protein. The malformed valine has been traced to a widespread source of GMO soy protein used in animal feeds as well as soy-based meat substitutes.*

"*When this defective valine is consumed directly from*

plant-based sources, as it is by livestock, it becomes part of the protein structure, making it unstable. That's why livestock are dying off from what appears to be premature old age, and why animal-protein products now have such a short shelf life.

"When the defective valine is consumed secondarily, as from consuming the meat or other by-products of these affected animals, the valine affects this particular gut bacteria and so triggers the chain of events leading to severe aggression. We'll bring you more on this important story as additional information becomes available.

"Meanwhile, the CDC and the USDA advise that you do not consume any beef, dairy, poultry, or pork products. Also, do not eat any GMO-based soy-meat-substitute products. These products will be recalled immediately from grocery shelves and destroyed, and you should throw away any such items you have in your home. Back to you, Erin."

The camera shifted back to the telegenic news anchor. The smile that usually graced her face had disappeared entirely.

"Thank you for that report, Ben. In related news, demand for wild-caught seafood has risen sharply, along with vegetables, beans, rice, and nuts. Not only have the prices risen, but shortages are anticipated due to unprecedented demand. We'll be your first news source when the CDC comes out with more detailed recommendations."

Marty gaped at the television. How could he possibly stay in business with his stock dying off and now with the government banning all animal-based products?

Not only that, but what was he—or anyone—supposed to eat? Everyone he knew out in farm country ate what they produced: animal products. Dinner was steak, pork chops, chicken, not a bunch of frilly vegetables. Nothing made a finer meal than meat he'd dressed himself. He'd slaughter a steer for himself every so often, cut it up into steaks and roasts, then put it in the big chest freezer in the basement. Usually lasted him quite a while.

He chugged the rest of his bourbon and got up to get himself some more. A lot more.

CHAPTER 33

Jim "the Fox" Sullivan was a happy man. A vindicated man. He'd been saying for years that fucking with Mother Nature was a crime, and someone would eventually pay. And yet, despite all the letters he'd sent to whatever nincompoop happened to occupy the White House, no one had listened. Maybe they would *now*.

Yeah, not only had they bungled the environment in general, but they'd gone and screwed with the food chain. Bad enough all the genetic engineering with the animals themselves, but they'd managed to really fuck things up now. They'd fucked up a basic component of soybeans, of all things, something that is fed to damned near any farm animal you can name, and now look what happened.

He shook his head as he thought about the news that had broken earlier in the day. It was a heavy burden being right all the time. Too bad he was right *this* time. There was already a world of hurt going on with all the violence, but now that the cause had been uncovered, there would be food shortages like nothing before. They were already starting, in fact.

He gazed out the window from the second story of his farmhouse. As far as his eye could see, nothing but livestock untouched by GMO-polluted feeds, antibiotics, and other BigAg Trojan horse products. Everyone who lived and farmed in his enclave held the same beliefs. That's why they followed him. That's why they lived the way they did. Clean and pure.

And that's why they'd always have enough food to eat. Nutritious and safe food.

The Fox smiled. He looked forward to the next town meeting.

His followers were already fiercely loyal to him, but with this new development, they would see just how wise they'd been to renounce their previous lives and follow him.

CHAPTER 34

Daphne lay on the couch, hugging Agnes close and trying to let the cat's rumbling purr soothe her and distract her from her pain. She'd closed all the shades and curtains in her apartment, plunging it into an artificial twilight that matched her dismal mood. Her cell rang, jolting her out of a half-sleep and causing Agnes to hiss and leap from the couch.

"Hello, Ms. Mercer? This is Dr. Adams from Mayo."

She already wished she hadn't answered her phone. "Yes?"

"I got the test results back on the Second Nature samples you brought me. They're consistent with yesterday's CDC announcement. The valine molecules are reversed, mirror images of what they should look like."

Daphne still wasn't sure she'd fully grasped the CDC's announcement. She closed her eyes and rubbed them. A headache couldn't be too far in her future. "So, what does that mean?"

"Apparently, the defective soy-based valine disturbs protein synthesis. It's causing livestock to age prematurely, and it's causing the drop in shelf life for animal-protein-based products. That problem soy is in livestock feeds—*and* it's used in the Second Nature products. Probably in other brands as well. If you eat enough of it, the defective valine in the soy gets incorporated into the structure of the proteins in your body, like skin and muscle, and weakens them."

"Great, so what can I do about it now?" The headache was gathering behind her eyes and preparing to strike with vicious force. No doubt about it.

Dr. Adams hesitated. "We're in uncharted territory, but

here's what I'm thinking. I don't see a quick fix, unfortunately. You need to consume proteins that contain normal valine. No animal- or soy-based proteins are safe—or even available—so that leaves mainly legumes."

"I'd be happy to do that, but I hear the prices are already shooting up. I hope I can afford to eat enough of them."

"There is another problem."

Daphne's stomach churned. "What?"

"Time. Not only do you need to get adequate levels of good valine into your system, but you also need to process it into properly formed proteins throughout your body, eventually replacing all the improperly formed proteins based on the bad valine. That takes time, and for you it will likely take longer than it would otherwise. The bad valine has compromised most of your bodily functions because of the accelerated aging process that it's already set up."

The dull throbbing spread from behind her eyes to her forehead and temples. "What are you saying?"

"I'm saying it will take time to halt the accelerated aging process, let alone reverse it." Dr. Adams let out a breath before continuing. "You're far enough along that I'm worried there may not be enough time left."

Daphne bowed her head and clamped her eyelids shut to hold back the tears.

After a lengthy, uncomfortable silence, Dr. Adams cleared his throat. "Ms. Mercer, I am truly sorry. I have to be honest with you about your condition. That said, none of my colleagues, nor I, have ever encountered anything like this. My concerns could be overblown. But in the meantime, begin supplementing your diet with legumes right away, and throw out any Second Nature products you may still have."

"Sure, thanks."

Daphne hung up and glanced at her watch. The grocery store would still be open. She pushed herself up from the couch and went into the bathroom to swallow some ibuprofen.

She forced herself to scrutinize her reflection in the mirror. Anyone could easily mistake her for a seventy-year-old now. A network of deep lines crisscrossed her face as if she'd spent years lying in the sun without sunscreen. The whites of her eyes were anything but, with their fine red lines and a slight yellowish cast. Streaks of gray shot through her long, dry, brittle hair. She turned her head slightly and wondered if she detected the slight whitish reflection of cataracts.

Daphne pulled into the grocery store's parking lot and nearly retreated in panic. Every single spot was taken and cars circled around like sharks hunting prey. She'd never seen the place so busy, even on the biggest sale days. She hated crowds and traffic, but figured she had no choice but to tough it out and buy all the legumes she could get her hands on.

After about twenty minutes of frantic circling and near misses, she got lucky and snagged a spot. She got out of the car, took a deep, calming whiff of the slightly cool mid-September breeze, and made her way into the store.

The inside was no better than the parking lot. Slow-moving shoppers clogged the aisles, uncertain as to what to buy now that their normal dietary world had been turned on its ear. She only had to make one change: to get her protein from sources other than soy products. Everyone else had to learn how to live without myriad animal-based products that made up the typical diet. Or used to.

Daphne grabbed a little basket and struggled past the tangle of people to get to the pasta and rice aisle, which would also have lentils and other dried beans. The effort, combined with being constantly jostled by other shoppers, sparked pain in all her joints, and her headache had not abated. She took deep breaths to fend off the dizziness that threatened to overcome her.

She finally arrived at the shelf she needed, only to find that precious few packages of beans remained. And those that remained had been marked up. Ten dollars each.

Daphne didn't want to think about how much higher prices would likely go, at least for the foreseeable future. She clenched her jaw, snatched the remaining four packages, and headed for the checkout as quickly as the crowd allowed.

CHAPTER 35

Stu Walters, CEO of Cornucopia Technologies, had faced numerous corporate crises over his long career with the BigAg giant, but never anything quite like this. He didn't believe the joint CDC/USDA announcement blaming faulty valine molecules for the unprecedented break in the food chain. At least, he didn't believe it until he received the results from Cornucopia's internal investigation. Somehow, at some point, their line of GMO soybeans had developed the mirror-image valine molecule. No one had ever considered the possibility that something like that would happen, so there'd been no checks in place to catch it.

And now, the entire inventory of the soy in question—seeds as well as processed meal and all related by-products—had to be destroyed. Cornucopia would have to start all over developing a line of soy that contained properly formed valine—no small task. He expected it would be quite some time before Cornucopia's soy division recovered.

Let alone the food chain itself. Livestock of every kind—beef, dairy, pork, poultry—were dying prematurely. All animal products, even eggs, milk, and cheese, had been declared dangerous to consume and had been pulled from store shelves, as had all soy-based meat substitutes. The commodity markets had collapsed overnight. He needed some big ideas and he needed them now, or he could count on Cornucopia going under. He'd be damned if he'd let that happen under his watch, no matter what it took.

Stu grabbed a pen and pad from his desk drawer, then headed down the hall to the conference room where his senior management team awaited. A palpable wave of tension hit him as he stepped into the room. Their grim faces left no doubt that his team fully grasped the gravity of the situation. He took his seat at the head of the long mahogany table.

"Let's get right to it, shall we? What about the immediate effects?"

Jamie London, the CFO, cleared her throat. She looked pale and uncharacteristically shaken. "My team's drilling down into the projections right now. I can already tell you it's going to be bad, and it's going to hurt for multiple years. We're likely to lose two or more crop years while we're reengineering our soy lines. As you know, the soybean division is—*was*—our largest and most profitable division. We'll lose half our revenue overnight."

She shook her head and gazed down at her papers before continuing. "I'll check with the tax attorneys about cushioning the blow with write-offs, but we need to somehow replace that revenue in the interim or Cornucopia may never recover."

Stu's shoulders slumped. "Wish I could say that surprises me." He turned to his chief counsel, Anne Freeman. "What about liability?"

She rested one hand on her legal pad and gazed at him with the poker face she wore in difficult conversations and in court. "We're still investigating to be sure we're not missing anything, but we do have some preliminary answers. So far, it appears we're not in too bad a shape from a liability standpoint. Of course, we won't be able to perform on our supply contracts, but our standard contract limits our liability to simply refunding any advance payments if we're unable to perform due to some event beyond our control."

Stu frowned. "But could someone say our production methods created the problem, and therefore it *was* within our control?"

Anne's expression betrayed nothing. "That's certainly possible, so we've already drafted language to refute such assertions if they materialize in the form of contract claims. I'm more concerned about negligence claims for damages resulting from the *use* of the products, like livestock deaths, damage to farming operations, and the like. The potential monetary liability for tort claims is far greater than under-contract claims, in my opinion. Now, we believe we can assert that such injuries were not foreseeable, and so can craft an effective defense on that basis. Of course, even with a strong position at the ready, there's still the expense and hassle of responding to the lawsuits, likely in multiple states."

Stu was glad he had a top-notch, aggressive legal team. He'd hired the best and paid them well. If anyone could handle a slew of suits over this mess, they could. "Thanks, Anne. So what do we do going forward? We have a problem here not just for our bottom line, but for the food supply as a whole. Ideas? Is there any way we can turn this into an opportunity?"

Ken Barnes, head of product development, finished making a note on his pad, then leaned forward and spoke. "You bet. We already have a small aquaculture division. You know, fish farms. They've not been on soy-based feed, so they're in the clear. We can ramp up that division quickly. That's a nearly immediate win-win. Gives the population a source of safe animal protein, and it capitalizes on an underutilized division."

Stu weighed the idea for a moment. "But some people don't like fish, and there's been some negative press about Frankenfish."

Eric Regan, head of marketing, set down the pen he'd been fiddling with and grinned. "Oh, I think we can change their minds readily, given every other source of animal protein just disappeared overnight. When there's no beef or poultry available, fish is going to look mighty good. It'd be a slam-dunk campaign."

Ken cut in. "And there's more. We can engage the Biotech division to work on new food products. They've been tinkering with some ideas the last few years, but not aggressively pursuing them. When the usual animal-protein products were available, the potential products didn't look all that appetizing. But now … things have changed overnight."

"What sort of products, specifically, are you thinking about?" Stu loved a good, rare steak more than about anything, and wondered what could possibly substitute.

Ken stood and began to pace around the table. "Lab-grown

muscle tissue. Beef. It still has a ways to go, but this could be the time to put serious resources into it." He stopped and smacked his fist into his palm. "Also, the Biotech division makes a liquid-diet substitute. You know, for when someone can't eat solid food for a while after, say, a serious facial injury or stomach surgery. The product provides complete nutrition without a feeding tube or IV arrangement. Obviously, if it's to be marketable for broader use, it'll have to be made more appealing."

Eric made a face. "That could be a bit more challenging to promote."

Ken turned to him. "Oh, I don't know about that. We could come up with some better flavors, an appealing product name and packaging. We could sex it up. Think about it. It provides all the nutrients you need; it has a long shelf life. Think of all the time spent preparing meals that could be saved using something like that. What could a person do with all that extra time?"

Eric smiled and nodded. "I see what you mean. That does have some possibilities." He laughed. "Sure you don't want to transfer over to Marketing?"

Everyone in the room broke into guarded laughter at Eric's remark, including Stu. He felt somewhat encouraged by Ken's proposals and Eric's enthusiasm for them. He just hoped there wouldn't be a backlash of consumer distrust, given that it was *their* soy product that started the whole problem.

But then again, Cornucopia Technologies was the dominant player in both BigAg and BigBiotech. The food problem was real and it was happening now. Only Cornucopia was positioned to develop and produce new products in the needed timeframe and volume. While it was a matter of do-or-die for them, it was probably only a matter of *die* for their smaller competitors.

Stu smiled. He never would have thought to create this crisis intentionally, but, handled correctly, it did present a fine opportunity to thin the herd and put Cornucopia on top for years to come. Out of an apparent calamity would come success beyond anything he'd ever imagined.

CHAPTER 36

Officer Jim Styles shifted uneasily on his horse. He reached up and adjusted his helmet's chin strap, even though he had done so seconds ago. He reached down and, in compulsive sequence, touched the gun, the pepper spray, and the handcuffs on his belt. A rookie cop, this was his first protest and he was nervous, even if he would never dare admit it to any of the other officers.

Protests—many of them violent—had spread across the country, most of them taking place in major cities. Word had come down that there would be a street protest in Seattle today, most likely in Pioneer Square, and so a contingent of officers on horseback was stationed at the International District bus stop, waiting.

"Let's go. It's starting." The lead officer waved his arm and led the way down South Jackson Street on his tall bay gelding.

Officer Styles nudged his horse and followed, his heart hammering and his mouth dry. He'd done well in his training, graduating near the top of the class, yet he still felt unsure of himself. The protest might stay peaceful, but what if it got out of hand and turned violent? What if he couldn't control his horse? He wondered if he'd chosen the right profession as his horse calmly carried him toward Second Avenue.

As the mounted officers rounded the corner and proceeded down the street toward Occidental Park, the crowd increased in size, seemingly from nowhere. The chanting grew so loud, Officer Styles couldn't hear himself think. He recoiled, wanted to run, to escape the wall of agitated, angry sound that pushed against him like a physical thing.

Protestors shouted in unison, "GMOs have got to go! GMOs have got to go!" The crowd continued to grow and mill around, swelling to fill the street and sidewalks. Traffic ground to a halt as protestors waved hand-painted signs and blocked the road.

"Shut down Cornucopia!"

"Prison for those who destroyed our food supply!"

"Let 'em eat their own poison soy!"

"No more GMOs!"

"GMOs destroy your brain!"

"Back to real food—if you can find any!"

Officer Styles closed his eyes for a moment and tried in vain to calm himself. An adrenaline rush like nothing he'd ever experienced before began to course through his body. His heart pounded; his breaths came in a staccato rhythm. Every muscle tensed, poised for action. He snapped his eyes open again. The crowd seethed along Second Avenue, but was—at least so far—doing nothing threatening, just chanting and holding signs.

A new sensation washed over him as he took in the sight. Something more than an adrenaline rush. A feeling of incredible strength, and a taut feeling of wanting to do something about it. Normally mild-mannered, he wondered what might be happening to him. Maybe it was nerves, but it felt like something much more serious, something alien.

A protester came toward him, waving a sign that said GMOs WILL KILL US ALL! and chanting "GMOs have got to go!" The sight of the man—his hair shaggy, his mouth open wide, his sign raised high—triggered something in Officer Styles, something he didn't know existed within him.

A sudden rage out of all proportion swept through Officer Styles like a wildfire devouring tinder-dry brush. A reddish glow tinged his vision as something vicious pumped through him and took over. Almost of its own volition, his right hand drew his gun, then aimed. The protester dropped his sign, held up his hands and stumbled backward onto the pavement. He tried to scuttle away, out of the line of fire.

Officer Styles pulled the trigger, and the protester's head blasted apart in a satisfying spray of red. He smiled, then aimed at the other protestors and fired until he emptied his gun.

The crowd exploded into action. Some ran screaming, bashing into others in their desperate attempt to flee. Others reacted differently. They attacked those around them with whatever they had available: fists, knives, and guns. Officer Styles climbed down from his horse and joined them.

Until a bullet slammed into the back of his head.

CHAPTER 37

Gretchen cringed on the couch, clutching a wriggling Lara in her arms and sinking back into the cushions as if trying to physically avoid his words.

"I'm afraid."

Kyle stood before her, his professional training at war with his personal feelings. They all needed to be tested. Immediately. And action taken, depending on the results. Lara didn't understand, but Gretchen did, and she was justifiably terrified. Hell, *he* was terrified. What if one or more of them tested positive? What then? He pushed aside those thoughts. He couldn't let *feelings* keep him from doing what he knew had to be done. The question had to be answered, whatever the cost.

"I know, I know. But we have to find out. We have to know the answer—for all of us."

Gretchen's face twisted as she fought back tears. "But we're not eating animal products anymore, not even any soy. We stopped right away when you figured out what was going on, even before the public announcements and recalls. Isn't that enough? Didn't you say once the harm was done, it was done? So why bother testing? What's the point?"

"We've got to know if any of us harbors *metasonis*, even though we've stopped exposing ourselves to the problem foods. There might be a latent period—a little slice of time—before the permanent harm is done. If any of us has the bacteria, I want to eliminate it with antibiotics. If it's possible to head off the damage, I want to do it."

"Are you insane? I'm five months pregnant! You of all people should know I can't just take things, not without possibly harming the baby." Lara began to cry, so she held her closer and tried to shush her. She glared at him and spoke in a tense whisper. "We nearly lost *her*. I can't bear to risk losing another baby."

Kyle sighed and sat on the couch. He had to get past her objections, so he put his arm around her shoulders and held her and Lara close. "Don't you think I know that? It's a risk we'd have to take if you tested positive. God knows we've all been exposed to animal products that *will* cause the problem in anyone harboring that strain. Not *if*, but *when*. The only possible way to avoid the permanent brain change is to eliminate the bacteria before it emits the chemical, if that's even possible at this point. It's our only shot."

Gretchen wiped away tears with the back of her hand and sniffled. "I can't believe this is happening."

"I wish it weren't, too. Believe me. Maybe we'll all test negative. That's entirely possible."

"I hope so."

"Daddy, why are you scaring Mommy?" Lara rubbed her eyes and sobbed.

Kyle leaned over and planted a kiss on his daughter's forehead. "Oh honey, I'm not trying to scare Mommy. We're talking about something important, is all. We need to check something out, and we may have to take some medicine. Or maybe not."

Lara made a face. "I don't like medicine. It always tastes *baaad.*"

Kyle gently ruffled her hair. "Don't worry. If you have to take any, I'll make sure it's your favorite flavor."

Lara smiled. "Okay, Daddy." She giggled and buried her face in Gretchen's neck.

Kyle stared off into space as he held Gretchen and Lara and tried to comfort them. He'd give anything for them all to test negative. But he knew each of them had a nearly one in two chance of testing positive.

He didn't like those odds, and he didn't like that he was likely chasing a sliver of opportunity that didn't even exist.

CHAPTER 38

Daphne swallowed a couple of ibuprofen, leaned back on the couch, and closed her eyes. She didn't like taking the stuff at all, but now her joints and muscles hurt so much all the time that she nearly lived on it. It probably didn't much matter. She'd been eating all the legumes she could manage in the past several weeks in a desperate effort to replenish her body with properly formed valine. But she didn't feel at all better, at least not yet.

Pain and exhaustion had forced her to cut back and serve only breakfast at the café. Business had been so paltry at lunchtime, it didn't hurt her revenue much, and it was a relief to decrease her work hours and be able to nap when she needed to.

Agnes slinked in from the kitchen, hopped up onto her lap, and gazed up at her, blinking her luminous green eyes. Daphne ran her hands through the cat's thick fur and tried to take some comfort from the soft vibration of her purr. Agnes was the only bright spot in her life right now. Her health was ruined, her business was in the toilet, and she got the cold shoulder from all the meat-eaters in town.

Daphne glanced at her watch. Somehow dinnertime had rolled around without her noticing. She wasn't hungry and didn't feel like getting up off the couch to try to make dinner. Maybe later. For lack of anything better to do, she clicked on the television to check the evening news.

Splashed across the bottom of the screen was the moniker of the day: CRISIS AT THE DINNER TABLE. *Leave it to the media to brand a catastrophe.* Daphne frowned, wishing someone could turn back the clock and unwind all the damage. If they hadn't tinkered with the soy in the first place, none of this would have happened. She wouldn't have been dying of old age before her time. Livestock and farm animals wouldn't be dropping dead and taking farmers' livelihoods along with them. And the wave of violence—both taking and ruining lives—would never have happened.

And now, in an effort to stave off more harm, a major portion of the food supply was off-limits. The few safe substitutes like fish and legumes were getting harder to find and what little that was available went for prices that many people couldn't afford anyway. Someone, at least, was making a handsome profit.

She watched, sickened, as the reporter narrated video of the latest repercussions of the crisis.

"Gun shops report a brisk business these days. As you can see, demand is so great that lines often extend around the block. Sales volume is so high that the gun registry database has crashed multiple times. Of course, that causes more delay and longer lines."

Unable to take any more, Daphne angrily clicked the remote and tossed it aside. She clung to Agnes as she hung her head and wept in the early evening gloom of her apartment. Not only for herself, but for the massive destruction the GMOs had brought on so many levels. Would a solution be found, or would this be the beginning of the end of the world?

CHAPTER 39

Ranger Mark Dixon pulled his rig into the parking area at Caprock Coulee in Theodore Roosevelt National Park. He lowered his window and breathed in the fresh morning air as he watched the sky take on the pinkish glow of a new day. Mark loved this park, had been a ranger here for fifteen years. If you'd asked him a month or so ago, he'd have said he wouldn't trade his job or his life up here for anything.

But that was before the food bans. Since then, there'd been pressure to allow hunting in the national parks, something he found to be nothing short of blasphemous. So far, the powers that be hadn't given in, but he worried it was only a matter of time. People were getting desperate for sources of unadulterated animal protein, and people voted. Pols cared about their votes far more than they did national treasures like native wildlife.

In the meantime, there'd already been incidents in Yellowstone and the Grand Tetons. Evidence that people had been sneaking into the parks, either under cover of darkness or simply when the gates weren't actively staffed due to budget constraints.

Bad enough they were hunting on national parklands, but they weren't even competent hunters. Carcasses of buffalo, deer, and elk had been found in varying conditions. Some had only been injured, and so escaped the hunters only to die slow, agonizing deaths later. Some had been killed more efficiently, their hacked-up carcasses left behind to rot when the hunter only took what little could easily be carried.

In response to the problem, park rangers nationwide had all been equipped with guns and bulletproof vests and provided hastily prepared training on how to handle themselves in potential confrontations with armed intruders. Mark scratched at the edge of his vest where it chafed his shoulder. He hated being made to feel like some street cop, but it made sense to be prepared for anything these days.

A loud report sounded through the coulee, setting off a blast of adrenaline through Mark's bloodstream. He strained to hear the echoes to try to pinpoint where it might have come from, then stepped out of his rig and scanned the horizon in the direction of the sound. Nothing visible.

He pocketed his keys, drew his gun and tried to breathe slowly to settle his hammering heart. There were no park visitors around at this early hour. Until he'd heard the sound of gunfire, he'd thought he was alone in the peaceful dawn.

Glancing from side to side, he proceeded along the trail in the direction of the gunshot. He wished he could call for backup, but the other rangers weren't scheduled to come on duty for another hour or so. He'd have to handle this himself and hope his training would carry him through. He never dreamed he'd ever have to deal with something like this.

Mark followed the trail along the edge of a formation of bentonitic clay, gray and textured like elephant hide. He knew the park well, had been on most of the official trails as well as most of the backcountry. He'd have that much of an advantage, but through this particular area, there weren't many places to hide.

The ground began to rumble with the sound of hooves. Heavy. Had to be buffalo. He stood still until he could figure out which way they were coming from. He knew better than to get in the way of a herd of panicked buffalo. Moments later, he saw them come blazing out from behind a set of formations to run right across the road and into the canyon on the other side, leaving an enormous dust cloud in their wake. He waited for the last of them to pass, then began walking in the direction from which they'd come, all his senses on alert.

He peered around the edge of a smaller clay formation, gun at the ready. About ten yards away, a man of medium build dressed in blood-spattered khakis knelt next to a downed buffalo. He wielded a large butcher knife and was hurriedly field-dressing the animal, his back toward Mark.

Mark hesitated, stunned and disgusted by the scene before him, a scene he never thought he would see in his park. The buffalo—all the wildlife—were protected. He'd only ever come across wildlife dead from natural causes or from being hunted by other animals. The man who'd shot this animal had demonstrated he knew how to use his gun.

Mark's mouth had gone bone-dry with fear. He licked his lips, raised his gun, and carefully drew closer. The hunter didn't yet know he was there. He wanted a better look, to see where the hunter's gun was, and he wanted to give the hunter the least amount of time possible to react when he did reveal his presence.

He crept forward a few more steps, carefully placing his hiking boots to avoid making any sound. The hand holding the gun began to tremble, both from the effort of holding the weapon up and from the jangling of his nerves as he watched the hunter gutting the buffalo, casting aside the organs as if they hadn't just been part of a living, breathing majestic animal. He gripped the gun with both hands now.

Mark tried to weigh his options. The longer he took to confront the man, the more things could happen during the delay. But once he challenged him, he'd better be ready for anything. He didn't know what to expect the man to do, and that ate at him as much as the sight of the desecrated buffalo. He took a deep breath and held it for a moment.

"Park ranger! Put your hands up over your head!"

The man glanced in his direction, but remained in a crouch. He smiled, his teeth appearing blindingly white in contrast to his thick, scruffy black beard. He said nothing.

"Stand up! Hands up! Step away from the buffalo!"

Still smiling, the man stood, raised his hands, and backed away from his kill, his left side toward Mark.

Mark breathed slightly easier when he saw that the rifle remained on the ground next to the buffalo. "Keep stepping back. What's your name?" He started to approach the man as he moved farther from the buffalo, one step at a time.

Mark was about ten feet away when, without a word, the man swept his right arm down, drew a handgun and fired. The movement was both blindingly fast and deathly slow.

The bullet slammed into Mark's neck, just above the edge of the bulletproof vest. He couldn't even scream as he lay on the ground of his beloved park, writhing in pain as his blood pooled on the earth beneath him.

CHAPTER 40

Gretchen slumped on the couch, feeling as tired and achy as if she'd spent the entire morning chopping wood. She and Lara had both been in slow motion since Kyle left for some all-day meeting in St. Paul. Their low-protein diet in the weeks since the ban on animal products had sapped their energy. Precious amounts of fresh fish could be found in the small Midwestern town, and the price of dried legumes had spiked. Lara turned her nose up at them anyway, no matter what Gretchen did to make them palatable for a three-year-old.

Kyle had warned her of what to expect from such a low-protein diet. She was pregnant and Lara was a growing little girl, so they both had higher protein requirements than Kyle and would be affected first. She glanced around the unkempt room. He was right. Normally, she wouldn't let things pile up like that, but she was just too damned tired all the time to do much of anything.

She watched Lara playing on the floor—if you could call it that. She seemed content to hold Baa-Baa and stare off into space much of the time. Her lustrous blonde hair had dulled and become brittle, like a cheap wig. Her bright blue eyes had an almost vacant look, as if the spark had gone from her. She didn't even look like the same child. Gretchen turned away from the sight. They'd nearly lost Lara once, and now she was slowly slipping away again. And there was not a damned thing they could do about it.

She blinked away tears and looked down at her hands. She'd always had such nice strong nails. Now they were ragged, chipping and tearing at the slightest provocation. Her hair had begun breaking and thinning. If her crappy diet was already affecting her this much, she didn't want to think what it was doing to her unborn baby.

She glanced at Lara again, angry and frustrated to be powerless to properly care for her. If only she could get some fresh milk. Lara loved milk and it would give her the protein she needed to grow and thrive properly. But even the nasty powdered stuff had been taken off the market because it, too, contained the faulty valine.

She leaned back and closed her eyes. Another one of those vicious headaches was starting up again, stabbing at her temples—yet another side effect of her shitty diet. She'd been getting them frequently these days, but she tried to avoid taking aspirin or ibuprofen because of her pregnancy. If only she could sleep for a while. But even sleep had been elusive lately.

Gretchen rubbed her dry, gritty eyes and opened them, then glanced at her watch. Lunchtime. She sighed. There was nothing all that enticing in the house to eat, and even if there were, she didn't feel like preparing it. Maybe if they went out for a while in the nice weather, it would help perk up their spirits, if nothing else. It was that sweet time between late summer and early fall that could be so beautiful in Minnesota, when the harshest of the heat and humidity is gone, yet the temperature is still pleasant and the trees are starting to get a tinge of fall color.

That was it. They'd go out for a little lunch. Maybe that vegetarian café over in St. Joe. It was a short drive, and if anyone could prepare nutritious vegetarian food that tasted good, it was that woman.

"Come on, Lara. Let's go get some lunch."

The little girl stared at her.

Gretchen took a deep breath and prepared herself to break the inertia for both of them. She pushed herself to her feet with a grunt and reached for Lara. "Come on. It'll be good for us both."

Gretchen pulled up to the curb. The lights didn't appear to be on inside the café. She frowned. A handwritten sign hung in the window, but she couldn't quite read it from the car.

"Let's go check it out." She got out and retrieved Lara from her car seat in the back. They walked up to the window together.

CLOSED FOR LUNCH UNTIL FURTHER NOTICE. WE ARE OPEN FOR BREAKFAST FROM 8–10 A.M.

Gretchen sighed. The owner had complained that she lunchtime business was slow. But that was then. Now that animal products had been summarily removed from everyone's diet overnight, she should be flooded with business. Seemed foolish not to take advantage of the opportunity.

"Aren't we going to eat, Momma?" Lara rubbed her face as if she were ready for a nap.

"Not yet. Let's stop at the store and see what we can find." Gretchen pursed her lips. A simple trip to the grocery store had become a stressful undertaking these days, with shoppers competing for the dwindling supplies of fresh foods and legumes. Unfortunately, the grocery stores were the only game in town.

Only a few weeks ago, they could've stopped at any of a number of fast-food places and found something they'd like. But all the fast-food joints, like all the other restaurants that had focused their menus on animal products, had shut down seemingly overnight.

A new kind of ghost town had emerged.

CHAPTER 41

Marty Janssen glanced around his cramped kitchen table at the grim faces of the half-dozen farmers assembled for the meeting. And grim they should be. They had to do something or they would all lose their farms. There could be no doubt of that. If he were more of a conspiracy theorist, he'd have thought BigAg cooked up this whole mess on purpose, but they seemed to be scrambling, too, so maybe that wasn't the case.

Paul Gorsham, his closest friend, sat to his immediate right. He flexed his knotted, arthritic hands and grimaced. "I think we're all here. Might as well get started."

Marty noticed that Paul's hands seemed to have worsened quite a lot lately. He felt a pang of sadness to see his old friend in pain. "Right, Paul. Well, I've been reading up on this thing extensively, and I don't see an end in sight. Even if we had viable, uncontaminated stock that would be allowed to go to market, we'd have nothing safe to feed them, at least for the foreseeable future. So what do we do?"

"Fish. Farmed fish," Paul offered.

"Switch over to aquaculture, you mean?" Marty tried to gauge the group's response. They were all leaning forward, attentive but silent. Whatever they came up with, they'd have to be in it together to make a go of it, so he hoped that was a good sign.

"Yep," Paul continued, "I've had no other great ideas, so I've been looking at what it would take to get started farming fish. There's stock available, and the feed they require isn't soy-based, so that's also readily available. For a price, anyway. But then there's the infrastructure: the tanks and filters and all the equipment to house 'em. It would be an expensive proposition to start, but have you seen what fish is going for at the supermarkets lately? That is, when you can get it at all."

Marty had indeed seen it. Thirty bucks a pound for local walleye. Anything from out of state, even catfish, was going for even more than that. If they could produce stock locally and avoid the transportation costs, they might be able to price competitively and still make a decent profit.

"That's interesting, Paul, but those start-up costs worry me. I think we should look at things that fit into our existing infrastructure. Maybe we could grow other sorts of beans than soy, like lentils. Those have been in high demand these days as a source of protein."

A short, aged farmer with a creased, weatherworn face spoke up from the far end of the table. "I don't have the money to dump into any fancy new infrastructure, so I like your idea, Marty. I'm sure the suppliers'll hose us for the starter seed stock. Nothing you can do about that, but we could set aside our own seed stock for the next year's planting if it works out." He folded thin arms across his gaunt chest. "Fish farming on the prairie. That's crazy." He let out a derisive snort, then chuckled and shook his head.

The other farmers nodded and started chatting among themselves. They were a cautious lot. No surprise to that. Even Marty wasn't wild about taking his chances with fish farming. But he couldn't go down without a fight. With Ellen gone, all he had left was the farm.

He decided to risk it. He could trust Paul as a business partner. Maybe they could go into it together. If it failed, it failed. At least he would have tried. The bank could have the damned place if it came to that.

And if it came to that, the bank could have his body, too. He'd have nothing left if he failed. Nowhere to go. No one to turn to. Nothing.

"Marty? What do you think?" The older farmer had again spoken, and the rest of them turned toward Marty, awaiting his answer.

"Huh? About what? Sorry, I was thinking about something else."

"We're going to switch over to legumes. No one here has the money to risk on fish. Too much up-front investment for a crapshoot."

Marty glanced at Paul. "What do *you* think?"

Paul stared down at his hands for a few moments as he smoothed them flat on the kitchen table, then shook his head. "I know the fish idea is quite a leap, but I don't think switching to legumes is going to be enough on its own. I'm gonna talk it over with Susan. She's the one who keeps the books and knows exactly what we have left."

Marty tapped Paul's shoulder, leaned over, and whispered, "Let's talk later. Maybe we can join together or something."

Paul nodded and answered quietly. "That might work. I'll get back to you."

Marty addressed the group. "All right, unless anyone has something else to say, I think we can wrap up this meeting."

He watched as the men stood and prepared to leave. They patted each others' shoulders as they shuffled out and said their good-byes. It was a good group, true enough. A little conservative, but that was understandable. They put their livelihoods on the line every year they farmed, with Mother Nature being a fickle mistress and market prices being mostly out of their control. It took a certain kind of person to live that life—and now they'd had their mainstay income flows shut off overnight. Even the worst farm disaster usually ruined only one year's production.

This catastrophe challenged their survival on a level they could never have imagined, let alone foreseen. Marty wondered who would be left this time next year.

CHAPTER 42

"Fish, you say?"

Paul nodded. "Fish."

Susan clutched her mug of hot coffee in both hands, sat back in her chair, and gazed at her husband across their kitchen table. Paul was usually about the most practical, play-it-safe man she'd ever met. That's why she loved him, and why they'd gotten along so well all these years.

"Why fish?"

Paul leaned forward, the hint of a gleam in his eye, and explained what he and Marty had discussed at the meeting last night. "The others are going for alternate legumes, like lentils. They have a point. No added infrastructure, but I think there's more of an upside potential in fish. Once we get past the start-up costs, of course."

"Fish." Susan opened the ledger that lay before her on the kitchen table, scanned the numbers, and pursed her lips. "You're right. We can't keep up like this for much longer. We do have enough cash on hand to go halves with Marty on the setup expenses, but not much more."

"I know it's a risk. I'm scared, too. But I think if we don't do something, we'll lose the farm this time for sure."

Susan closed the ledger, then stared down at it as she ran her fingers along the worn cover. Dad's ledger. The entire financial history of the farm since he bought it back when he first married Mom.

"It's just, well, even though Mom and Dad are long gone, I'm afraid to let them down, to lose the farm they worked so hard to establish, you know?"

Paul reached across the table and took her hand. "I know." He smiled. "I'm sure your dad wouldn't be too keen on us taking a chance on fish farming. He was a good man, but as old-school as they come."

"You say Marty's been researching this already?

"Yeah, extensively."

"He's no fly-by-night himself. If he's looked into it, I'm sure he's been thorough. God knows he's resourceful enough, keeping that place going all alone after Ellen died and the kids moved away. Of all of the others, he's the one I'd feel most comfortable partnering with."

"So you want to go for it?"

Susan gazed at Paul. He'd never let her down—not in any way—in all these years. She trusted he wouldn't start now.

"Let's do it."

CHAPTER 43

Kyle felt almost physically ill, burdened with what he knew and what he had to tell Gretchen. He'd *had* to order the tests. Now he wished he could undo what he'd learned. But that was impossible. He knew what had to be done, and what it would likely mean. And he knew despite the terrible price, it might not even work.

He stood silently outside Lara's room and watched Gretchen put her down for her nap. He loved those two more than anyone in the world, and he couldn't bear to witness what the food bans had already done to them. It was like watching them die before his eyes while he stood by, helpless to get them the foods they needed to maintain their health. Lara had become so thin and lethargic. And Gretchen. She looked exhausted, between caring for Lara and struggling through her second trimester.

Of course he was glad he'd found the root cause of the violence epidemic. But the solution created its own devastating problems. Malnutrition had become widespread thanks to the lack of adequate, affordable dietary replacements for the animal-based food products—and even the soy substitutes. Children and pregnant women were the most vulnerable, the ones who would suffer the consequences the fastest.

He'd heard that the Biotech divisions of the Big-Ag corporations were all hard at work trying to come up with new products to fill those dietary gaps. But they weren't available yet, and there was no estimate when they would be. He hoped that when they did come out, they didn't create new problems.

"Oh, you scared me!" Gretchen pressed her hand to her chest, turned to make sure Lara hadn't been disturbed, then closed the door behind her. "How long were you standing there?" she whispered.

"Oh, only a moment." Kyle touched his hand to her shoulder. "We need to talk."

Gretchen paled and frowned. "About what? As if I don't know."

"I got the lab tests back. Come sit down. You look dead on your feet."

Gretchen followed him into the kitchen and took a seat at the breakfast table. "It isn't good, is it?" She twisted her hands together and avoided eye contact. "All right, who has it?"

Kyle wondered if there was any way to soften the blow, then decided that wouldn't be possible. "Only one of us has it, and it's … you."

Her eyes wide, Gretchen put a trembling hand over her mouth. "Oh my God. But the baby."

Kyle dared not tell her the baby was the least of his worries. Her gut bacteria had likely already secreted the chemical that would cause the permanent changes to her brain, and she wasn't yet symptomatic. He had to hope he was wrong and the damage somehow wasn't already done. The only weapon he had was antibiotics to kill the *B. metasonis* as fast as possible, and they could not allow the fetus to stand in the way of that one slim chance to save Gretchen from becoming a violent psychopath.

"There's no choice. We have to eliminate the bacteria. Immediately." He took a vial of pills from his pocket. "You need to start on these, right now."

Gretchen leaned back in her chair and stared at the vial as if he'd asked her to drink a bottle of arsenic. "No, I don't want to—"

Kyle put his hand on hers. "You have to. Believe me." He got up, filled a glass with water and set it down on the table in front of her. "Three times a day for the next ten days. If you'd rather, we can do it by injection. If you won't—or think you can't—take the capsules, then we'll have to do it that way."

Her face red and tears streaming freely, Gretchen reached for the vial and picked it up gingerly. She read the label, then opened it, removed a capsule and placed it on the table in front of her. She stared at it for several moments, as if gathering her nerve, then popped it in her mouth and washed it down with the water.

Kyle had chosen to withhold one terrible piece of information. The antibiotic he'd given her was the only one effective against *metasonis*. It also caused fetal death. He didn't want Gretchen to feel any more guilt and worry than she already did. There was simply no other choice to try to prevent her from becoming a dangerous, violent maniac.

He hoped it worked.

CHAPTER 44

Doug Townsend never imagined he'd end up in a situation like this, lurking in a dark alley on the outskirts of Kansas City. Like some goddamned dope dealer. But he had to do it to survive these days. That's why he did it. It wasn't money for luxuries or crap; it was money he needed to live. To feed his kids, his wife. Himself.

He checked his watch. Nearly time now. He hoped the package wasn't getting too warm while he waited in the darkness. The night was cool and comfortable, but he'd been waiting for maybe a half hour with the package tucked under his arm like a precious prize.

And indeed it was. To someone, anyway. Someone willing to pay dearly for it.

Doug kept his eye on a curbside spot beneath a busted streetlight, the rendezvous point he'd agreed on with his customer. He wanted to be able to pop over to the car, get his cash, deliver the goods, and disappear quickly and quietly into the night. There was a penalty these days for doing what he was doing.

Moments later, a gleaming black late-model Mercedes pulled up to the agreed-upon spot. His customer. Doug glanced from side to side and, seeing no one else around, moved quickly to the passenger side of the car and leaned down. The window lowered, revealing the driver, a clean-shaven man who looked to be in his fifties, dressed all in black. Doug could see no one else in the car.

"You have it?"

"Right here."

The man's hand reached into his shirt pocket and then extended out toward Doug. In the hand was a stack of hundred-dollar bills. Doug grabbed them and quickly counted. Ten. He handed over the package.

"Thanks."

"Thanks." The man raised the passenger-side window and drove off into the night.

Doug pocketed the money and hurried back to the side street a block over where he'd parked his pickup truck. He got in, relieved to be done with his clandestine errand, and began the forty-mile trek back to his farm.

Jeff McClain reached over to the passenger seat and rested his fingers on the package as he drove back to his home down in Fairway. He frowned. It wasn't exactly warm, but it didn't seem properly chilled. He hoped it hadn't been compromised by a lack of refrigeration. He pressed the accelerator harder, pushing the Mercedes as fast as he dared. A speeding ticket would be bad enough, but he didn't want to get caught with the package.

A short while later, he pulled into his garage and shut the door. Anxious to see what a thousand bucks bought these days, he went straight to the kitchen, took out a plate, and set it on the charcoal-gray granite counter. Then he tore open the package, rinsed off his prize, and placed it on the plate.

It was gorgeous. A well-marbled, bright-red, inch-thick ribeye steak. Just like you used to be able to buy at any good meat counter only a few weeks back. Before beef was outlawed overnight because of the panic over the food supply.

Jeff was born and raised in the Kansas City area, and he loved nothing more than a prime, locally produced cut of meat. He'd had to search long and hard to find someone willing to supply him under-the-table, as it were. For a rather hefty price. Good thing he could afford it, at least for now.

He eyed the steak closely. It looked perfect in every way. His supplier claimed he never used soy-based feeds, that he'd only ever fed his herd grass and hay. He hoped that was true. But right now, he was willing to take the chance. It's not like he ate it every day—especially at these prices, and with having to sneak around like a common criminal to even get it.

Worried the steak hadn't been kept as cool as it should have been, Jeff decided he'd better cook it up now for a late dinner, rather than risk any problems re-refrigerating it. He poured himself a glass of Cabernet and considered making a side dish. A baked potato would be perfect, but he didn't want to wait an hour for it to roast in the oven. And a microwaved potato would be blasphemous. Screw it, he'd just have the steak, and enjoy the hell out of it.

He flicked on the outdoor deck light and glanced at the stainless steel gas grill that stood out there, lonely and neglected of late. He shook his head. It was a shame with a steak like that, but he didn't dare cook outside and risk someone catching a whiff of it. They might report him to the police, for all he knew. He'd better play it safe and broil it indoors.

He turned off the deck light, went back to the kitchen counter, and turned on the broiler to preheat. Then he opened his spice cabinet and considered all the little bottles and jars. A steak like that needed only simple seasonings to enhance its flavor, so he ground fresh black pepper over it, then sprinkled a little kosher salt and thyme on it. He popped the steak into the broiler, then leaned back against the counter, sipping his wine and savoring the aroma while the meat cooked. It seemed like such a long time since he'd been able to enjoy that smell.

When it was done, he slipped the steak onto his dinner plate and gazed down at it, taking in the beauty of a perfectly prepared cut of meat. He went into the dining room, set his plate down at the head of the table, and lit a candle. Then, after settling himself in his chair and having another sip of Cabernet, he cut into the meat, pink and rare. Ruby-colored juices flowed from the rest of the steak onto the dish as he took that first bite, savoring the texture and flavor of real, prime beef. Too bad it had become so hard to come by.

CHAPTER 45

Les Anderson reached into his refrigerator and cracked himself a cold beer after a long day of what had become the new normal for him: euthanizing all sorts of livestock dying from premature aging, starvation, and often both. So now, instead of making calls to vaccinate herds, assist births, perform artificial insemination, and all the other things he normally did in his years of practice, he found himself attending to what appeared to be the beginning of the end of small- to moderate-sized ag operations in these parts.

He plunked himself down at his tiny kitchen table and stared at the worn grain of its unfinished wood surface as he took another long swig of his beer. He'd gone to vet school to learn how to heal animals and keep them healthy. Euthanasia was a last resort, an admission of either failure or the inevitable. But it's about all he did these days. He was helpless to cure the stricken animals, to solve the problem by anything other than destruction. And he didn't see things turning around anytime soon.

Everything seemed to be deteriorating around him. His livelihood, his eyesight, his ability to do anything useful anymore. Maybe it was getting to be time to retire. He'd had a good run as a vet. Why keep on making calls to watch the end of non-corporate ag as he knew it? He took another sip of his beer and shook his head. It was too damned depressing to think about.

Les glanced up toward the kitchen counter, at the faded blue curtains hanging lopsided on loose rods. Remnants of Tammie. After the wedding, she'd furnished and decorated the place in a whirlwind of enthusiasm. She'd been so proud to have married the town vet. But she must have envisioned a far more glamorous and exciting life than he'd been able to give her.

She'd never managed to comprehend how he could come home each day stinking of piss, shit, and blood, and yet feel satisfied with his day's work. She'd never understood what it meant to him to have the power to heal animals, and nothing he did or said ever changed that. He shrugged. Obvious now they were never meant to be. He never did understand why decorating the house was so damned important, and so the place still looked the same as when they'd married. Only older.

Right now he was too weary even to give a shit about what to make for dinner. Fish didn't appeal to him, although he figured he'd better get used to it. He sure as hell wasn't into those bean-based conglomerations they touted as protein substitutes. To him, they tasted nasty.

But it was a new world, and who knew when farmers would be able to produce meat, milk, and eggs the way they used to. Meat, milk, and eggs that wouldn't screw up your brain, that is.

Les downed the rest of his beer, got himself another, and took it into the living room. He parked himself on his threadbare couch and flicked on the remote. And regretted it immediately. Even on mute, it was clear what the top news story was. Again.

Panic in the streets. In all the major cities. All those people so removed from what it was like to work a real-life producing farm. They were used to getting their food all nicely cellophaned in the market and now they were up in arms to see meat cases that were darkened and empty. They'd been hoodwinked into thinking their readily available meat and animal products would always be safe and plentiful. Now they were neither.

"Idiots," he muttered at the TV.

So you had the panicked people, wondering how and what they should eat in this new world, and you had the angry people who just wanted to scream and yell about it. They wanted someone to blame. He could understand that, but as a practical person, he didn't think it mattered now. What mattered most was how the hell to rebuild the industry on safe footing. He had no idea how long that would take, or how it would be accomplished. But it surely wouldn't happen overnight.

All those people parading around with their signs, sparking violence in those already predisposed because of the damage wrought by the screwed-up food chain—well, they weren't accomplishing anything. They were making it worse. He hated the waste of it all.

Les clicked off the television, chugged the rest of his beer, and then decided to have a bit of the harder stuff tonight. It's not like he was going to get a call to attend a breech birth or something. Death could wait.

CHAPTER 46

Daphne grimaced as another sharp pain spiked through her lower back. She rubbed the knotted muscles with one hand and stirred the various meals-in-progress on her grill with the other. *Two sides to every coin,* she thought. The valine scandal and all it had spawned had forcibly and dramatically changed everyone's eating habits overnight. People no longer had the choice to eat unhealthy—and now deadly—animal- and soy-based products. And because of that, they were flocking in desperation to where they could eat nutritious, balanced food that wouldn't kill them or destroy their brains.

The irony was not lost on Daphne as she surveyed the bustling café from her vantage point in the kitchen. Though her menu items were easy to prepare, it still took all her energy to get through the day and handle the crowds. Fortunately, demand for her meals was such that she could charge way more than she imagined possible and sock away a nice profit. Good thing, too, because her suppliers had raised their prices substantially, and sometimes she didn't get her deliveries because they ran out of stock. Then she had to be extra creative with what she had left on hand to keep her customers satisfied.

Despite following her doctor's instructions to the letter, Daphne felt her health slipping away a little more each day. So she didn't dare pass up the opportunity to make some good money while she still could. In fact, she'd begun to wonder just how long she'd be able to keep the café going.

More customers arrived, forming a line that snaked out onto the sidewalk. They'd have to wait for a table to open up. Daphne shook her head. The way business had been when she first opened her café in this meat-obsessed town, she'd never dreamed her little place would ever be standing room only.

Daphne gazed out the front window. The midday light had begun taking on that wistful sort of look that only comes with autumn. She'd always loved that light, so beautiful and pathetic at the same time. She pressed her lips together and fought off tears. Her own health was fading like that autumn sunlight.

And that sunlight wouldn't last much longer.

CHAPTER 47

Jim "the Fox" Sullivan threw his head back and laughed at the TV news report. He laughed with his entire body, convulsing from head to toe and stopping only when he began to choke. He wiped the moisture from his eyes, cleared his throat and took a few deep breaths to recover from his excessive mirth.

Molly hurried in from the kitchen. "What's so funny, Dad? Must've been something good." She perched herself on the arm of the couch and took a bite of her sandwich.

Every time the Fox looked at his daughter, tall and healthy and beautiful, he knew he'd made all the right choices. Moving out here to establish his enclave when she was a little girl, and leaving that airhead mother of hers behind in the city. Molly had grown into a smart young woman, and he could envision her running the place some day.

"Did you hear the news report just now? It's happening. It's all happening as I predicted, only worse. I've always said GMOs would destroy the food chain, and that's exactly what they've done."

Molly smiled. "You were right, and I'm glad you were." She held out her roast beef sandwich. "*Our* food won't kill us. I can't imagine what it's like not to be able to trust what you eat." She shivered and took another bite.

"Yeah, it's crazy out there, with people killing each other. Damned GMOs have wrecked their brains. They've pulled the dangerous stuff off the shelves, but without a Plan B. So now everything's going to hell."

"What's happening now? I couldn't hear the TV from the other room."

"Oh, people fighting in the aisles at grocery stores, shooting wild animals in the national parks. Restaurants closing, farms failing, unemployment going through the roof. And widespread malnutrition."

Molly frowned. "God, it's like the total collapse of everything."

"Yep, they screwed the pooch but good this time. Broke the food chain and the economy—as well as allegedly civil society in general. Just shows what lurked beneath it all, doesn't it?"

"They should've listened to you. Everybody here's happy and healthy, with plenty of good, safe food."

The Fox shrugged. "They had their chance. I can't tell you how many letters and emails I've written to how many presidents over the years. None of them had the courtesy to even respond. Treated me like some crackpot. Idiots didn't listen, and now look what's happened. If they'd read my manifesto, the country—the world, for that matter—wouldn't be turned on its ear right now."

Molly finished her sandwich and stood. "Well, how about a nice thick steak for dinner later?"

"That sounds great. I'll be plenty hungry by then." The Fox clicked off the television, rose from his well-worn recliner, and went out to the mud room to prepare for his afternoon farm chores. His enclave's way of running their farms may be considered old-fashioned, even quaint. But it got the job done and *they* were having the last laugh now.

Thanks to his brilliant planning, of course.

CHAPTER 48

Ted Warner was a born worrier. But unlike most worriers, he was a man of fearless action. That combination made him a natural for his job as head of the Department of Homeland Security. He could think of doomsday scenarios better than anyone he knew, better than any way-out novelist. And he was as good at solving problems, no matter what it took.

For years, he'd figured something would happen to the Homeland's food supply to create a national emergency of epic proportions. Granted, he'd expected the root cause would be terrorism, not some screw-up, but the result was the same: panic in the streets, economic and social turmoil. He shook his head. Terrorists couldn't have hoped for better, had they been behind it.

No matter. He'd come up with a plan to get the ship righted again. He already had some ideas. And absolute authority to implement them. The president preferred it that way—plausible deniability if Ted had to do something a little unorthodox to get the job done. Yet another reason he loved his job. He'd been able to implement plenty of new programs to keep the Homeland safe, and no one ever got in his way.

Someone knocked on his office door. "Come in."

In stepped Alex Russell, head of the USDA. Ted noted with satisfaction that he was right on time for their meeting. Punctuality pleased him. He took it as a sign of the respect due a man with his power.

"Have a seat."

Alex sat in the guest chair, arms folded across his chest and an uncertain look on his face. His posture came as no surprise to Ted. The very name of his department tended to intimidate people. It conjured up all sorts of images in their minds—many of them quite sinister.

"I know you have a lot going on right now, so I'll get right to the point. I'm working on a response to the food-chain crisis, and I wanted to check with you on a couple of assumptions before I put the plan into action."

Alex frowned and spoke hesitantly. "Sure. What do you need to know?"

"The way things stand right now, I see two closely related problems. First: the soybeans. The inventory of all existing soy— both beans and soy-based products—had to be destroyed, and seed lines that don't harbor the faulty valine molecule need to be reestablished, is that right?"

Alex's frown deepened. "Yes. I've been in close touch with the key BigAg players, and they all agree the fix is perhaps a couple of years out, and then of course we'd be a couple of years' harvests away from having anything close to a working inventory of actual soybeans."

"So the only way to shorten that up would be to already have a line of seeds known to be safe—there'd still be the need for multiple harvests after that to reestablish sufficient inventory, yes?"

Alex shifted in his chair. "That's right. There may be some farmers out there with small supplies of safe soy seeds. But the GMO versions had become so popular because of their rapid growth and weed resistance that they mostly squeezed out the non-GMO versions."

"Okay, and the second problem is the livestock supply. Once we have safe feeds that won't re-create the problem, we need to develop livestock lines that haven't been exposed to the bad soy feed, right?"

Alex's shoulders slumped and he let out a sigh. "That's right. It's really a knotty problem. Until there's a safe line of soy, there isn't much to feed any livestock anyway unless we start diverting corn from ethanol production. Though with fewer people driving, demand for ethanol has dropped, so that may be more possible now than it would have been a few months ago."

Ted noticed a slight tremor as Alex ran a hand through his wavy brown hair and continued. "But there are likely only small pockets of unaffected livestock to begin working with anyway. The popularity of that all-in-one soy feed made sure of that."

Ted couldn't think of any other questions for Alex. He'd learned what he needed to know to move forward. He stood and extended his hand.

"Thanks, Alex. That was helpful."

"You're welcome." Alex hesitated and opened his mouth as if to ask a question, then pursed his lips and left without another word.

Ted wrote down a list of the team members he wanted to conduct the operation he had in mind. He only needed to work through a couple of remaining logistics items, brief them, and they'd be ready to go.

He loved his job. Every problem had a solution. You only had to recognize it and not be afraid to get it done.

CHAPTER 49

Stu Walters recognized the look on Ken Barnes's face. He'd seen it before, when Ken had a new product in the pipeline and had a good feeling about it. He hoped that was the case today. He'd called Ken and Eric Regan, his head of marketing, into his office to discuss progress on the lab-grown meat product.

"So Ken, how's it going?"

"Things are moving along." He leaned forward in his chair, his arms and legs restless with energy. "I think we're going to have a near-term and a long-term solution."

"How so?"

"We're close to production-ready on the simpler version, the one we were already working on before the crisis. It'll be fairly easy to produce, but it's only available in, well, sheet form. That's because we use a flat-matrix base to maximize the surface area for nutrient distribution. The muscle tissue grows quite readily on that."

Ken sat back and chewed on his pen for a moment before continuing. "On the one hand, this is an inferior version of the product I would prefer to produce, but in light of the crisis, it may be more palatable to consumers in the near term than it would have been otherwise."

Sheets of beef tissue didn't sound terribly appealing to Stu, even though a good steak already seemed a distant memory. "Aside from the form, how is it?"

"I'd say the flavor's close to naturally produced beef, maybe a little milder. The texture's as similar as it can be, given its quarter-inch-thick profile. This version doesn't re-create the depth and grain of a natural steak, or the marbling. We inject it with fat cells to give it moisture and flavor."

The corner of Eric's mouth twitched down. "That sounds a lot like the Frankenbeef design that consumers rejected in surveys. Could be a hard sell, even under the circumstances."

Ken gave him a sharp look. "I'd love to hold off releasing it until we had a more natural-looking design, but we don't have that luxury. There's a dearth of complete protein substitutes out there, what is available is going for sky-high prices that people can't afford, and malnutrition is already becoming a big problem. Consumers have few options available. We need to put something out there to take advantage of the opportunity."

Stu nodded. "I agree. Cornucopia's bottom line needs something *now* to help stop the bleeding—and consumers need an additional source of complete protein in the food supply. What's the ultimate plan for the product, Ken?"

"I have a separate team working on that right now. Version 2.0 will use a more complex, three-dimensional matrix structure, much like artificial capillaries that will carry nutrients to the muscle tissue as it's being grown in the lab. We'll handle marbling in a more sophisticated way, too. We're aiming for a more natural-looking cut of beef, nearly indistinguishable from the real thing."

Eric smiled. "That's more like it. I can see that being a real winner, especially if it's a long time before safe lines of natural cattle can be reestablished."

Stu tried to ignore a sudden desire for a thick, rare steak. "And speaking of safety, have you run the necessary tests on Version 1.0?"

"Yes, we've been testing extensively. The valine is properly formed. In fact, we've verified that *all* the amino acids are properly formed. We're taking no chances with this, none at all."

"Good. We might end up with some profitable new products out of this crisis. That's some consolation, I suppose." Stu still worried that the soybean division might bleed enough to take down Cornucopia Technologies in the end, but maybe they could still mitigate the losses. He stood. "Thanks, guys. Keep up the great work. I need to get ready for my next meeting."

He didn't look forward to his meeting with his CFO, Jamie London. He'd probably need a good, stiff drink after that one.

CHAPTER 50

Jack Rawlins kept one eye on his semi outside and one eye on the cashier as he paid for a bottle of full-caffeine Coke and a bag of ranch-flavored Doritos. He was glad there were only a couple of other customers hanging around.

"Thanks, man."

He grabbed his change and hustled back outside into the bright fall afternoon. The longer he left his rig unattended, the greater the danger. He'd stopped for gas, then took care of business and got his snack in the C-store in record time. He glanced around to make sure no one was watching him, then quickly unlocked his rig, got in, and relocked the door.

Jack set the chips aside for later, opened his Coke and took a good long guzzle before capping it and setting it in the holder. He wiped his mouth with the back of his hand and belched. Then he opened his glove compartment and glanced at the handgun he kept in there. In all the fifteen years he'd been trucking cross-country, he'd never felt the need to arm himself. But things had changed. You could run into a crazy anywhere these days.

And with the way things were, he might as well be transporting a load of pure gold from Fort Knox. A few months ago, he'd never imagined a truckload of farm-raised catfish could make him a target. But now it did, and he had to deal with it. So he'd bought himself a gun, took the necessary training, and got his concealed-carry permit last month. He slammed the glove compartment shut. You couldn't take any chances.

Jack started up his rig and eased it out onto the road. He glanced at his GPS. On a nice clear afternoon like this, he ought to be able to make it to Olathe, Kansas, in about four hours. He'd decide where to stop for the night when he got closer to Olathe. He wanted to avoid stopping in Kansas City if he could. Larger cities worried him. He felt more secure staying at a small-town motel where he could keep his rig within view of his room.

After a few blocks, he took the on-ramp and pulled into traffic on northbound I-35. Jack worked his way up the gears, settling into cruising speed. Not too fast, not too slow. He glanced around. Traffic was moderate, and the GPS didn't show any particular jams ahead. He relaxed a little in his seat and took another swig of his Coke.

Jack switched on the radio and flitted among the stations until he found one playing country music. He liked listening to local stations. The commercials gave him a feel for the places he drove through. He tapped his hand on the wheel in time with the song that was playing. That was the best part of driving—other than the pay—being out on the road by himself, the rumble of his rig and the radio keeping him company.

Something disturbing in his side mirror caught his eye. A huge pickup, maybe an F-250, was in the lane to his left, about seven o'clock from him. He could barely see it in the mirror, at the edge of his blind spot. He shifted his attention back to the road ahead of him. There was another semi a ways ahead of him, and a smattering of passenger cars in the other lanes. Nothing unusual for this time of day south of the Oklahoma-Kansas border.

But something didn't feel right. People who drove those huge pickups tended to be hot shots, not drivers content to travel at the limit set for truckers like him. Why was it pacing him like that? It'd been that way for maybe ten miles since he'd first noticed it. Jack pressed the accelerator, edging up his speed.

And the pickup stayed right with him in the same relative position, like its image was painted on his side mirror. A drop of sweat trickled down his temple. Jack glanced toward the glove box. He reached over, opened it, and put the gun on the seat beside him. He'd hoped never to have to actually use it, but it couldn't hurt to have it easier to reach if he needed it.

Keeping one eye on the road in front of him, he again stole a glance at the side mirror. The pickup suddenly flashed its lights and pulled up alongside him. Before he grasped what was going on, it swerved and clipped his driver front fender, causing him to stray onto the shoulder.

"Fucking asshole!" He jerked the wheel to get back on the road. The rig lurched from his overcorrection, and flung the gun and Doritos onto the passenger-side floor before settling back into the truck lane.

"Oh my God." Jack took several deep breaths to steady himself. He'd had a few emergencies in his life on the road, but nothing like this. He glanced again in the side mirror. The pickup was parallel with him, but had moved over a lane. He took another deep breath and let out a sigh. Maybe the driver was drunk, and had lost control for a moment. At least the thing was farther away from him now.

Bang!

The wheel jerked. Jack clamped his hands on it as hard as he could. Sounded like a gunshot, but it felt like his driver's front had blown out. The rig wobbled and swerved as Jack fought the wheel to regain control, but it was too late. The cab made a sharp left turn and the trailer tried to turn right. He closed his eyes and clung to the wheel as the truck jackknifed and rolled onto its side in the ditch.

Jack hung sideways in his seat belt and shoulder harness. All motion had abruptly ceased. One minute, he'd been rumbling down the road doing maybe sixty-five, and now his rig lay on its side, silent except for the radio that played on as if nothing had happened. He slowly opened his eyes.

Glass fragments from the ruptured windshield covered him and the inside of the cab, but he seemed to have gotten away with only minor scratches. The seat belt had kept him from smashing his head on anything. He carefully undid the buckle and released himself to stand with his feet on the ground beneath what had been the passenger door window. He heard voices outside. Someone must have stopped to help already.

"Hey, I'm in here!"

He elbowed the remaining safety glass away from the windshield's frame, crawled out of the cab, and then sank down onto the dirt next to his ruined rig. He felt light-headed from the shock of the crash.

"Shoot it! Get in there and start unloading!"

A series of gunshots rang out, followed by more shouting and the sounds of a commotion from the other side of the trailer, just outside his view. Jack struggled to his feet and staggered in the direction of the sounds. He reached the end of the trailer, gripped the edge in both hands, and peered around it.

Several men stood at the now-open back door of the trailer, hauling out boxes of catfish from the refrigerated interior and loading them into the pickup. As he watched, several other cars pulled over, their drivers and occupants spilling out to get their portion of the loot.

He staggered forward. "Hey! Put that stuff down!"

The closest of the men turned toward him, and in one fluid motion, pulled a gun from his waistband, raised it and fired.

Jack opened his mouth to scream, but never had the chance as the bullet blew his skull apart.

CHAPTER 51

Gretchen wept quietly as she gazed down at Lara's sleeping face. Her once-beautiful blonde hair had become as dry and brittle as the fake hair on a cheap doll. It fell out so easily, she'd had to stop brushing it. Lara's pale scalp showed through the ratty tangles that remained. Even her fingernails had become ragged and fragile. She looked unkempt, uncared for, and Gretchen was powerless to help her.

Lara looked like she was fading away by degrees, and Gretchen wondered how much more her little body could withstand. In the weeks since the food bans went into effect, the consequences of poor nutrition had ravaged her little girl—as well as her own pregnant body. She turned away from the heartbreaking sight and gently closed the door to Lara's room.

Another vicious headache clawed at her temples and made her queasy. She walked out to the living room window, opened it, and gazed down at the courtyard. The coming change of seasons announced itself by tinting the trees below with shades of gold and crimson. She inhaled deeply, relishing the fresh, crisp fall air. She wished fall could go on forever, but she knew snow wouldn't be far behind in this part of the country.

Gretchen absently rubbed her belly and wondered how much longer Kyle would need to work here. She worried she'd need to see an OB/GYN soon for prenatal checkups, that she'd already put it off too long. Maybe she could go back to her previous doctor in Minneapolis for the time being. It was a bit of a drive, but it might work, at least for her second trimester.

She went through the living room and kitchen and threw open all the windows. Maybe the fresh air would help clear up her headache without having to take anything for it. She made a wry face. As if it mattered, with the potent antibiotics she was on. The baby might already be damaged, so what harm could ibuprofen do? Still, just in case, she decided to try to forgo taking anything more.

Gretchen moaned softly as she lowered her weary body onto the couch. Maybe she could find some escapist daytime program to distract her from her worries for a while. She clicked on the television and was immediately faced with dramatic live-news helicopter footage from the scene of an armed robbery of a truck out in Kansas.

"Within the last hour, this truck had been headed northbound on I-35, transporting a load from a commercial fish farm down in Oklahoma. Witnesses say another vehicle tried to run it off the road. The driver apparently lost control and the truck jackknifed into the ditch. Someone shot the driver in the head and most of the cargo was stolen within minutes. Police are in a standoff situation trying to protect the crime scene and what little remains of the load. Details are still coming in. We'll keep you updated as we know more."

Gretchen stared at the television, openmouthed. About a half-dozen police officers stood there, guns drawn, guarding the overturned truck. A huge crowd surrounded them, right there at the side of the freeway, like they didn't care if they died trying to get to the cargo.

Afraid to see what might happen next, Gretchen clicked off the television. She couldn't believe people had become so desperate to pull off something like that. But then she thought of Lara, so innocent, sleeping in the other room, slowly dying of malnutrition. Maybe those people had starving children at home, too.

She put her face in her hands and wept.

CHAPTER 52

The early morning sun was tinting the world pink as Jim "the Fox" Sullivan tossed down several blocks of hay from the back of his flatbed truck. His cattle took notice and broke into a trot to get at their morning meal. He smiled as they tore into the hay. The Fox enjoyed getting up early to begin his farm chores. At dawn, the air was clean, the world was quiet, and the day was still a blank slate full of promise. He couldn't understand why more people weren't interested in a good, simple life like his.

Not everyone in his enclave was such a fan of early hours, though. Some would be out already, greeting the new day and tackling their chores. Some would get going a little later. But they all put in long days of honest work, producing good, safe food. He was proud of what he'd created out here.

The Fox had just gotten back into his truck to drive to the next pasture when something caught his eye. Something on the horizon of the hills that surrounded the enclave and gave it a private feel. What could it be at this hour?

He leaned forward and strained to see through the dusty windshield. Something was moving into view in the weak early light, coming into focus as it drew closer. His breath caught when he realized a convoy of dark-colored vehicles with tinted glass windows was headed toward the enclave. The look of them screamed *government*.

The convoy snaked down the dirt road that led right into the heart of the enclave. The vehicles in front looked armored, and appeared to be escorting larger, transporter-type vehicles. Dust kicked up around them, concealing some of the vehicles farther back. From the look of it, their intentions could only be hostile.

The Fox grabbed his cell, tapped out an urgent text, and sent it to the distribution list that included all the members of his enclave. In the message, he urged everyone to drop whatever they were doing, arm themselves, and gather at his place. And do it now.

He gunned his truck to get back to his house. First he had to make sure Molly was safe, then he had to arm himself and prepare to organize everyone when they arrived. Fortunately, his rifle had an extremely precise scope, giving him excellent accuracy, even at a distance. He'd need all the advantages he could get.

He pulled the truck up behind his house, hopped out, and dashed inside. Molly, her eyes wide and her face pale, stood frozen in the kitchen, cell phone in hand.

"What is it, Dad? What's going on?"

"Big convoy coming in. Looks like government. Heavy vehicles. You stay in here. I don't want you outside."

"But what—"

"I mean it. You stay in here."

The Fox left Molly standing in the kitchen. No time to lose trying to explain something he couldn't yet explain. He had to act. He hurried to the gun cabinet in his den, grabbed the rifle, and loaded it. Then he shoved a box of ammo into his shirt pocket and darted out the back door, positioning himself at a corner of the house to conceal himself from the approaching vehicles.

He watched from his hiding place as the transportation units came to a halt a little ways off and the vehicles from the front came closer, fanned out, and stopped. Armored Humvees. Had to be government. But what the hell did they want?

About a dozen members of the enclave entered his near pasture on foot, likely those who'd received his text while they were already out doing their morning chores. Too late, he realized his order to have them all meet at his place had become a trap, now that the Humvees had arranged themselves as they had.

He waved at his friends to try to warn them off. But before they could react, the Humvees, which had been running with their lights off, turned their headlights on high. The blinding light concealed the vehicles behind its intense glare. The Fox could only see his people caught in the dazzling light as they raised their hands to their eyes and staggered around, stunned and exposed.

That's when the shooting began. It all happened so swiftly, the Fox never even got off a shot. All he knew was that his friends were cut down in an instant, like rag dolls. He'd remained tucked right behind the corner of the house, safe from the line of fire. He heard a few moans, but they didn't last long. Whatever they were using for ammo, there was no standing up to it.

A few more stragglers came running toward his house from the other direction. He tried to wave them off before they caught the attention of the shooters, but it was too late. They, too, were cut down midstride.

The Fox backed away, farther behind the house and out of the vehicles' line of sight. The headlights cast a menacing glare on the bloody, shredded bodies of most of the enclave members. He hoped the younger kids had stayed behind, but he couldn't be sure, and he couldn't get a message out now. Those lying dead in the field would've had their cell phones with them, so he couldn't reach the kids now anyway.

Adrenaline churned through him, pushing his heart so hard he gasped for air. Light-headed, he sank to the ground to gather his wits. He tried to slow his breathing, to think. What to do? The shooting had stopped, leaving a terrible silence in its wake, but he had no doubt if he showed himself, he'd die in a hail of bullets before he could draw a single breath.

He snuck inside the house through the back door, then crawled across the pinewood floor to a front-facing window in the living room. He carefully raised his head and peered out a corner of the window with one eye, hoping no one would notice the movement.

The vehicles remained in place, ominously still. Whatever they wanted, they didn't yet have it. But if killing everyone in sight wasn't the end goal, what was? What would they do next?

If they thought they'd killed everyone, maybe he could at least hide out until they left. *If* they left.

He needed to check on Molly, but he didn't want to risk someone outside hearing him call to her from the living room. He quickly duck-walked to the kitchen, then fell to his hands and knees. He choked back a sob as he crawled over to her.

She'd been blown in half. Everything above the waist simply no longer existed. Her mangled lower torso lay twisted and mired in blood, tissue, bone fragments, and broken glass. He glanced up at where the window and part of the wall above the kitchen sink had been blasted open. Numb and on autopilot, he crept back to the living room.

The Fox remained frozen in place for the better part of an hour, watching, waiting for something to happen. His back ached from sitting in a rigid position, straining to see and not be seen. He saw nothing move from his vantage point, but he did hear more sporadic gunfire from farther off. Then more silence.

Finally, the forward vehicles dimmed their headlights and opened their doors. Heavily armed men dressed in black got out of the Humvees. They all looked bulky—probably bulletproof clothing. They had helmets with glass shields over their faces. Probably bulletproof, too. Fucking government.

They advanced toward his farm, slowly, each of them moving his faceless helmeted head from side to side, scanning for anything left to shoot, most likely. They got right up to the fence, still with their sniper guns at the ready and looking from side to side. Then one of them raised his arm in an apparent signal. The transports began to roll. They approached his farm at a slow rate of speed. As they drew closer, he could see they, too, had tinted glass and armor plates.

He glanced at his rifle. As fine a weapon as it was, he might as well have brought a pop gun to a war. He sighed. Nothing to do but stay hidden and wait it out. He crept across the floor and went to the bathroom window that overlooked the pasture at the side of the house. He cringed when he saw the bodies of all his friends, strewn there like so much bloody debris. Like Molly.

Then one of the transport vehicles drove up and positioned

itself next to his cattle chute. Two men got out. They were dressed in protective gear like the others, but did not carry guns. Instead, they each carried a small rectangular case. They slipped over his fence with practiced ease, set their cases down next to it, and began shouting and driving his cattle toward the chute.

After a few minutes of wrangling, they loaded one of his cows into the chute and blocked it in. Then one of the men went to his case, opened it, and took out what appeared to be some sort of medical supplies. He approached the trapped cow, his back to the Fox, and did something. Then he returned the items to the case and closed it. They repeated the entire process with a second cow before returning the cases to their truck.

The Fox tried to decide what to do—and realized his options were nil. They'd killed his daughter as well as likely everyone else in the enclave, and now they were doing something with his cattle as if they had all the right in the world. He didn't have the firepower to stop them, but he couldn't stand by any longer. He scuttled back into the living room, picked up his rifle, then took a deep breath to ready himself.

After a few moments, he rose to his feet, squared his shoulders, and strode to the front door. He waited a beat, then flung open the door, stepped outside and shouted, "Goddamn you fucking murderers, get the fuck off my property!" He aimed his rifle and pulled the trigger just before he felt an impact that punched him backward into the house with a deafening roar.

He lay on the floor, too stunned to feel pain, as darkness quickly and quietly took him away.

CHAPTER 53

Special Agent Ben Tucker leaned over and smiled. "You were wrong, Fox. We *were* listening all these years. We knew all about your operation out here, always have. But now the Homeland needs it more than you." He stood, hands on hips, and gazed down at the Fox. Or what was left of him, anyway. The body still lay, bloody and twisted, inside the house where the force of the bullets had blown it.

So far, so good. Phase One had gone according to plan. By striking so early in the day, they'd caught the enclave members mostly off guard, which made elimination fairly quick and easy. His frontline teams had scoured each and every house and outbuilding for any stragglers, and had reported none remaining.

Elimination was complete, and his teams were busy loading up all the bodies for transportation to a covert DHS location for disposal. It would be as if they'd never existed. Other team members were collecting additional samples, to be absolutely sure both animal and soy stocks were completely free of the faulty valine.

Phase Two would take longer. They'd brought equipment and supplies to secure the entire area from any possible passersby, so that in Phase Three, the enclave could be converted into a DHS installation to continue the existing ag operations in place.

Ben returned to his Humvee to make his status call.

Ted Warner hung up the phone and smiled. His team had carried out his orders flawlessly. They'd secured all the livestock—every cow, pig, and chicken—as well as all the soybean seed stock and dried harvested beans at Sullivan's compound.

Now they had a base livestock and soy inventory entirely free of the bad valine they'd use to speed up the eventual recovery of the food chain. It would probably be a year or so before their efforts bore sufficient fruit to be of value, but in the meantime, the necessary breeding and preservation operations would continue right in place at the compound under covert DHS control.

And they'd left no one alive to reveal what had taken place.

CHAPTER 54

Daphne awoke, her head pounding like something was fighting to smash its way out of her skull. The sliver of morning light sneaking past the bedroom curtain gouged her eyes like a dagger. She squinted and turned away. Every muscle burned without mercy, and she felt so weak. And so thirsty.

Agnes crept over onto the pillow and tried to nuzzle her, as if she knew something was wrong. She'd have loved to roll over and cuddle, to enjoy the comfort she usually took from Agnes's deep purr, but she had to get to the bathroom to take something for her headache. Now.

She tried to push back the covers, but only managed to partly free herself. Even that small effort drained her today, worse than usual through all the pain. She struggled to a sitting position and tried to swing her legs over, but the covers caught her and she toppled onto the wood floor. She landed hard and bit her lip. Warm blood seeped into her mouth, the taste of it nauseating. She wanted to go hang her head over the toilet until the feeling passed. Too weak to get to her feet, she started to crawl toward the bathroom. Agnes followed her closely, sniffing at her and yowling in alarm.

Daphne had closed the café entirely a couple of weeks ago because of her rapidly deteriorating condition. Cooking, serving the customers, sourcing the ingredients, and generally running the business took far more strength and energy than she had to give anymore. It was all she could do to cook for herself and Agnes these days.

When she'd noticed herself getting so much worse, she'd asked Dr. Adams what to try next. He'd told her as humanely as possible that he could do no more for her, and that she should start preparing herself for what now appeared inevitable. He'd offered to hospitalize her so she could be cared for in some degree of comfort and safety, but she'd refused. If these were her final days, the last place she wanted to spend them was alone in a cold and sterile hospital, without Agnes.

Now she began to doubt the wisdom of her choice as she dragged herself across the floor, inches at a time, desperate to get to the bathroom before she lost control and threw up—or worse. She reached out her right hand and tried to get some traction on the smooth wood floor. She pulled with all her strength. Nothing happened. Her body didn't budge, even as thin and light as it had become these days. She tried again, grunted, moaned. No closer.

Daphne glanced toward the bathroom door, so close and yet so far. She raised her head slightly and looked back. Her cell was on the nightstand. Unreachable. It might as well be on the roof. She squeezed her eyes shut and sobbed as she realized how utterly helpless and trapped she was. Too weak to hold up her head any longer, she lay face-down in a small pool of blood from her lip, mingled with tears.

A shattering pain ricocheted through her head. Dark spots danced in her line of vision and she felt light-headed, like she was going to faint. A searing pain shot through her chest and she gasped, suddenly unable to take in enough air. She tried to pound on the floor in case anyone might hear, but she couldn't even lift her arms.

Agnes snuggled gently against her and began to purr. Daphne closed her eyes and let the purring soothe her until it faded off into the distance along with the pain.

CHAPTER 55

Ted Warner steepled his fingers and leaned back in his chair as he considered what his department's medical expert had told him earlier. The food chain crisis had a public safety component that remained unresolved.

The CDC's epidemic investigation unit had done an admirable job in tracking down the root cause and pathology of the wave of violence that had plagued the Homeland. He smiled. Whoever had accomplished *that* was quite the investigator. But one problem remained: what to do about those persons who were affected?

From what he understood, these individuals formed two classes: those who'd already become violent and had been apprehended by some law enforcement agency—and those who *would* become violent. It was that latter group that had to be addressed, and quickly. It was the only way to stem the tide of violence and return the Homeland to relative peace and security.

No doubt any program to address that latent group of violent offenders would be costly. After all, as his medical expert told him, nearly half the population carried the specific gut bacteria that was critical to the causation chain. But given the stakes, he was certain he'd overcome any resistance to the cost.

The more difficult problem would be getting past resistance to the *nature* of what he would have to do. The liberal press and those civil libertarians would undoubtedly object and try to block the program.

Well, it wouldn't be the first time. Anyone who'd try to stop him from doing his job obviously wasn't a true patriot. *He'd* do whatever it took to protect the Homeland. Nothing was more important.

CHAPTER 56

Jenna Ames leaned against the hallway wall outside Lakeside State Hospital's main ward and tried to steel herself for the day ahead. If the past weeks were any indication, it would be another shift of pure hell on earth. She knew when she took the job several years ago that the place wasn't lavishly funded, and the residents were often abandoned, distrusted—even hated—by their families. But she believed their mental health issues were not their fault, and that they deserved humane treatment.

But that was then. The powers that be had made the hospital the dumping ground for all the violent offenders who didn't fit in the local jails. It made for a bad combination. Now the place was jammed to well beyond its intended capacity with both extremely dangerous offenders and actual patients. Beds lined each side of the wards, two deep.

For the sake of everyone's safety, the offenders were heavily medicated and restrained in their beds. The place had taken on the air of some medieval bedlam. Armed guards of questionable training and background had been quickly rented and stationed throughout all the wards. Jenna felt more like a prison assistant than a nurse specializing in the care of patients with significant, though treatable, mental health issues.

To make matters worse, the ban on animal-protein- and soy-based foods had severely affected the diet they could provide on an institutional scale. It was woefully inadequate in complete proteins and B-vitamins, and the effects were beginning to show in the form of muscle weakness and pain, headaches, sleep disturbances, and hair loss. Though she couldn't do anything about the poor nutrition, treating the resulting symptoms kept her all the more busy passing out additional medications.

She wondered how much more she could take. It was hard enough to face each day under such conditions, but it was made even harder because she, too, wasn't getting sufficient protein in her diet and had to fight through her own weakness and malaise to do her job.

Jenna sighed, then entered the ward before she could change her mind. She saw Katie Finch, the rookie nurse who shared her shift, already hard at work trying to get an elderly patient back into his bed. She hurried over to help.

Katie flashed her a quick and weary smile. "Hey, thanks, Jenna." Then she turned to her patient. "Now, Mr. Morgan, you need to get back in bed. You're not strong enough to be up and around."

"Those men have guns! Can't stay here!" Mr. Morgan spoke with the rasp of a long-term smoker. His eyes bulged, the whites tinged with yellow.

Katie turned her head and whispered, "Those guards. Just having them here scares the crap out of the regular patients, and only seems to goad the violent ones they've parked here. I'm not sure I feel any safer with them around, either."

"I know what you mean." Jenna scurried to the other side of the patient's bed to block his view of the guard. "It's all right, Mr. Morgan, you're safe here. Lie back down. You need your rest. Let Katie give you your medicine."

The frail man lay back on the bed, his bony hands and withered forearms raised over his chest in a protective position. "I'm not so sure. Reminds me of the war. Never safe in war, never be safe again." A single tear slipped down the side of his creased face.

Katie gently cradled his head and raised a tiny paper cup to his lips. "Here you go. Drink this little bit down. You'll feel better."

Jenna watched as Mr. Morgan turned to Katie with a cautious look and accepted his medication. She hoped he would rest and find a little peace once the mild sedative took effect.

A sudden noise changed everything. Jenna turned in time

to see the guard drawing his gun on the last patient in the row.

"What did you say, you sonofabitch? You lay back and shut up!"

His eyes wild, Mr. Morgan swatted away the paper cup. "I told you! Let me out of here!"

Katie flung her arms around her struggling patient in a desperate attempt to restrain him, even as she glanced over at the confrontation. "Oh my God, it's one of the guys the cops brought in."

Jenna couldn't believe what she was seeing. The guard stood there, legs planted, gun drawn. The patient, one of their more violent ones, was bound to his bed by both wrists and ankles. He raised himself, strained at the bindings, and screamed something unintelligible at the guard. "He must have palmed his meds or something. What the hell did he do to make the guard pull his gun?"

"What do we do?" Katie almost had Mr. Morgan wrestled down to the bed.

"I don't know!" Jenna tried to think of whom to call for help, and how to do it without escalating the situation.

Bang!

Jenna grabbed the bed rail for support.

Katie screamed. "He shot him—right there in his bed!"

Every patient in the ward reacted at once. Those who were restrained fought and writhed in vain to escape. Those who were only sedated struggled to get out of bed, many of them falling to the floor and howling in pain. A general melee broke out, with a chorus of panicked screams, from the patients and from Jenna and Katie.

The guard swept his gun from side to side, firing indiscriminately into the ward. He hit a number of patients, triggering more screams of terror, as he made his way toward where Jenna and Katie stood. Mr. Morgan cringed in bed in the fetal position, covering his head with his arms and whimpering.

He spotted them and halted. A hateful leer spread across his face as he took aim. *Bang!* Katie went down, an enormous puddle of red blooming around her on the linoleum. Jenna turned, slipped in the blood, and barely got out the ward door before she heard another round of shots. She ran as fast as she could to the nurses' station to call 911.

CHAPTER 57

A farm field lay before him, stretching into the distance as far as he could see. The vista was etched in stark black and white, not a hint of color anywhere. Even the sky cloaked itself in a toxic shade of gunmetal gray.

He glanced from side to side. Soybean plants, all in neatly arranged rows, starting in front of him and running off into the infinite distance up to the horizon. Nothing but the soybean plants. No houses, no buildings, no people, no animals.

All blackened and withered, as if charred from fire and left in place as silent witnesses to ultimate death and destruction. Poisonous, death-dealing black. The color of hopelessness.

Kyle jerked awake, gasping and drenched in sweat. His heart hammered so hard he could hear it beating inside his ears. He lay still and tried to calm his breathing so he wouldn't wake Gretchen. She hadn't felt well all day and needed her rest. He rolled over, adjusted his pillow, and tried to erase the nightmare from his mind.

Then he heard her moan. Softly at first, then she startled herself awake and let out a cry.

"What's the matter?"

"Oh God, it hurts." Gretchen spoke in a low, tight voice, strained by pain.

Kyle sat up and flicked on the bedside lamp. "Gretchen, what is it?"

She grimaced. "Cramping. I think it's contractions. Too soon."

Kyle had expected this to happen, given the side effects of the potent antibiotic he'd put her on. But the abstract concept of losing the baby was sterile and benign compared to the reality of watching Gretchen begin to experience it. A pang of guilt sliced through him with every sound she made, even though he knew full well he'd had no choice but to prescribe the drug.

She turned away from him, crumpled into the fetal position and barely stifled a cry of pain. "Something's wrong. I know it is."

"Let's get you to the ER." Kyle gently pulled down the covers and clenched his jaw when he saw the blood.

"I'm going to call ahead and get the car ready. I'll be right back for you." Kyle finished buttoning his shirt and left the room.

Pain like hot, vicious pincers gripped her abdomen, then released, in shorter and shorter cycles. Gretchen clutched her belly and held her breath when it hit, then panted for air in between the contractions. That had to be what it was. Premature labor, just like with Lara. Only earlier. Too early.

Kyle rushed back into the room and grabbed her robe. "Here. Let me help you into this, and we'll go."

"What about Lara?"

"I put her seat in my car, but I want to get you in the car before I wake her."

Gretchen clenched her teeth through another searing pain as Kyle gently helped her up and into her robe. "It's happening again. I know it. The baby's coming."

Kyle's mouth formed a grim, straight line. "Let's try to stay calm and get to the hospital as quick as we can. Walk with me."

Gretchen leaned on Kyle for support, one arm around his waist and the other arm across her belly. They made their way out of their suite and to the elevator, stopping every so often for her to breathe through the pain.

"All right. You rest there while I get Lara." Kyle shut the passenger-side door and trotted back to the front door of the hotel.

Gretchen leaned back in the seat, hands on her belly, and tried to take deep, calming breaths, but the jagged, recurring pains seemed determined to spin her into a panic. She clutched the door handle in a death grip and glanced around. The car was parked outside the bright pool of light coming from the hotel entrance. Something about sitting in the dark in a rented car, outside a hotel in a strange town, made her feel even more helpless and doomed.

A few minutes later, Kyle emerged from the hotel, cradling Lara in his arms. He opened the rear passenger door and strapped her into her kiddie seat.

She rubbed her eyes and fussed like she was about to cry. "Where are we going?"

"Just for a little ride, Lara. Mommy's not feeling well, so I need you to be quiet, okay?" Kyle put his finger to his lips and made a shushing noise.

"What's wrong with Mommy?" Lara's voice quavered with fear.

Gretchen turned in her seat as best she could. "It's okay, I just feel a little sick right now. You be a good girl for me, all right?"

"Ooookay." Lara yawned.

As they drove to the hospital, Gretchen gritted her teeth and forced herself to be silent each time the pain came, to try to keep from panicking Lara. She was glad it was only a short drive; she didn't know how long she could keep up the pretense.

They pulled up to the ER entrance, and then things started moving fast, everything whirling out of Gretchen's control. Kyle got out and ran inside, returning only moments later with an orderly and a wheelchair.

The orderly lifted Gretchen up and into the chair with amazing ease and whisked her to the ER, leaving Kyle and Lara behind. Just as quickly, Gretchen was scooped up and onto a bed. A nurse came, took her vitals, and fired questions at her. Someone started an IV in her arm. It all became a blur. Time had no meaning, but at least the pain had receded some, like a wave on the beach.

Later she realized she'd somehow been taken into another room somewhere else in the hospital. Bright lights hurt her eyes as she lay flat on her back in the bed. She felt like she'd lost track of something, like she'd been out for at least a little while.

A man dressed in green scrubs stood over her. He pulled the surgical mask from his face, letting it hang from its straps. He placed a hand on her shoulder and peered down at her with a face filled with sympathy.

"Mrs. Sommers, you're going to be okay."

She drew in a sharp breath and forced herself to ask the question she feared she already knew the answer to. "What about the baby?"

He shook his head. "I'm sorry." He straightened up. "I'll have your husband come in." He left before she could say anything more.

Kyle walked in and took her hand.

She snatched it away and glared at him. "It's *your* fault. I *told* you I didn't want to take that drug. I've been worried the whole time I'd have another preterm birth, like with Lara." She turned away from him. "I shouldn't have let you talk me into taking it, no matter what. Now our baby is *dead*! Leave me alone."

"Gretchen—"

"Get out of here! Now!"

Gretchen clenched her jaw until she heard the hospital room door close, then she pressed her face into the pillow and sobbed.

CHAPTER 58

Kyle slumped in a molded plastic chair next to Gretchen's hospital bed. After her angry outburst last night, he'd requested they give her a sedative so she could get some sleep and start healing. Thankfully for both of them, she remained asleep now. He hoped they'd both get a chance to rest and recover before picking up where they'd left off in the blame game.

He pawed at his eyes, scratchy from lack of sleep, then checked his watch. Seven o'clock. He had no appointments today, so he could concentrate on his family without having to make calls and rearrange things.

The night had been a horror for them all. Lara didn't grasp what had happened, which was just as well. When they'd arrived at the hospital, he'd had to leave Gretchen's side for a while so he could make arrangements for Lara. Fortunately, there was an empty pediatric bed she could use. A kind nurse and a mild sedative, and Lara at least had a safe place to be so he could focus on Gretchen.

Of course, the fetus was stillborn. Viability was a slim prospect as it was, given the stage of Gretchen's pregnancy. But in this case viability was impossible because of the grave defects caused by the antibiotic regimen—defects so severe, they hid them from Gretchen to avoid traumatizing her further. He wished he hadn't seen them himself. Nothing would ever erase that image from his mind. He would have to carry that burden himself, never *ever* revealing to Gretchen what he'd seen.

Kyle was relieved she didn't lose much blood and the doctors didn't expect her to have any lasting physical effects. With her compromised diet, it would take longer than normal for her to heal, but it would be far less of a drain on her than had she carried the baby to term and given birth.

He pondered that last thought a moment, and wondered what would have happened had he *not* prescribed the antibiotics. Would she have been able to withstand a full pregnancy—as well as the actual childbirth—with her compromised protein levels? Unless something changed, she likely would've been much weaker by that point. He glanced over at Gretchen's closed, sunken eyes. Terminating this pregnancy almost certainly saved her life.

Kyle somehow doubted she'd accept that, let alone forgive him. He envisioned a long road ahead before their lives returned to normal. If they ever would.

CHAPTER 59

D r. Lowell Adams set the autopsy report down on his desk, then reached up and rubbed his eyes. Nothing remarkable in the report. A death due to age-associated changes. Happens all the time. All systems generally compromised and failing. Specific cause of death: cardiac arrest.

Nothing remarkable—if the deceased were eighty-five or ninety years old. But Daphne Mercer had been only thirty. At least the results confirmed his diagnosis. But he'd been unable to help her.

The anomalies in her body's protein structures had been pervasive, and they exhibited no reversal whatsoever. He wondered if she'd passed some tipping point when simply consuming only normal valine could no longer cure the problem. Maybe the improperly formed valine and associated protein structures had become part of her DNA. That could be it. But what was that tipping point, and how many in the population had already consumed enough soy products with the faulty valine to exhibit the same effects as Daphne?

He shook his head at the irony. Daphne had been so concerned about her diet and adamant about avoiding animal-based products. Yet she'd unknowingly consumed products that turned out to be as deadly for her as for the livestock that consumed the bad valine in their GMO soy-based feeds.

He made a note to talk to someone at the CDC. There might be other cases like Daphne's out there, even though the products had already been pulled from the shelves. They should put out a public service announcement urging those who were heavy consumers of soy-based products before the ban to see a doctor immediately for testing. Not that there was likely any effective treatment for anyone as severely affected as Daphne.

Still, better for people to know, get evaluated, and at least be able to make their final plans as needed.

CHAPTER 60

Marty Janssen opened his back door. Paul Gorsham stood there, scowling and kicking the snow from his boots.

"Come on in. I just made some coffee."

"Sounds good, thanks." Paul stepped inside, took off his boots and hung his down jacket on a wall hook in the mud room.

Marty led Paul into the kitchen and motioned for him to sit. He filled two mugs with coffee and joined his friend at the kitchen table.

"I've been crunching the numbers on the fish farm operation. The startup costs are still weighing down our bottom line. Doesn't surprise me. The setup was a little trickier than I expected and I think we got hosed for the initial stock." Marty shrugged. "Kind of expected that, though."

"I've been going to the auctions, and fresh fish are fetching a good price. Once we have some product to sell, I think we'll recoup those costs quickly."

"Well, that's what we're hanging our hats on. Hope that demand keeps up."

"I think it will. There's talk of them coming out with some lab-raised meat, but I can't imagine that will catch on." Paul made a face. "Disgusting. Completely unnatural."

Marty shook his head. "Yeah, well, unnatural is what got us here, isn't it?"

"What do you mean?"

"The GMO soy in the feed. If they hadn't screwed with the soy, none of this would've happened."

"Right. I guess nothing's natural anymore." Paul stared

down into his coffee and warmed his swollen knuckles on the mug.

"Nothing we can do about it but carry on as best we can, my friend. So now there's the matter of the energy bill." Marty glanced out the kitchen window at the falling snow. "We insulated the setup well, but when it gets below zero, we'll see how much it's going to cost to keep those fish warm."

Paul turned toward the window and sighed. "Yeah. The whole idea of fish production in this neck of the woods is bold. Well, hopefully bold, and not *stupid*. I hope the heating costs don't torpedo the operation."

Marty watched the flakes fall and imagined them trying to smother their new business venture in its cradle. "I know. I hope we didn't jump right into a money pit with this idea. I know the others are laughing at us for trying to raise fish out on the plains." He sighed. "But we had to do something. We couldn't just lay down and die."

Paul nodded. "They can laugh if they want, but I don't know how the others will survive another year. Of course, we might go down in flames faster, given these startup costs." He gazed off into the distance and shook his head. "God, I hope this pays off. This is the only life Susan and I know. If our farm fails, I don't know what we'll do."

Marty heard the emotion in his friend's voice and glanced away to spare them both the embarrassment of such an uncharacteristically open moment. His eyes came to rest on the coffee mug Paul gripped in hands white with fear, knotted with arthritis.

They were all dancing on the edge of loss.

CHAPTER 61

Kyle slouched at his desk, catching up on emails while Gretchen made dinner and hung out with Lara in the kitchen. He'd spent the last couple of weeks meeting with local health care providers and agencies working out protocols for the diagnosis and management of those affected by the valine problem. He didn't yet know what his next assignment would be—or where it would be—and the wrap-up work felt like an odd limbo to him after the constant stress of the actual investigation.

Maybe the lack of protein in his diet was getting to him, darkening his mood. He should have been proud of what he'd accomplished, but he wasn't. The solution to the problem had brought nothing but misery, widespread malnutrition, and an economic tailspin. He'd prescribed a drug to Gretchen that had doomed their baby—and may or may not have helped her. He often found himself thinking it would have been better if he'd never figured it out at all.

Vic Rayburn had already put a letter of commendation in his file, and had promised to give him a glowing reference when he completed the program. Vic told him he'd be in high demand after what he'd achieved, and would be able to land the job of his dreams. Kyle pressed his lips together. Ordinarily, he'd be thrilled to no end. He loved epidemiology and wanted to excel in his time in the EIS program.

But the whole thing had taken a terrible toll on him and his family.

In the weeks since losing the baby, Gretchen had taken on a strange remoteness. He knew part of it was the resentment she still harbored against him, but he subtly kept an eye on her, worried she might also be slipping into depression. She still took care of Lara and handled the more mundane chores, but she seemed to be just going through the motions these days. He tried to give her the space and time she needed to heal and work through the loss, but he would need to intervene soon if she didn't start to improve.

He gazed out the window at the late November sky. Snow had begun to fall, and an early twilight was fast approaching. The short, frigid, and gloomy days of winter in Minnesota couldn't be helping Gretchen, either. Maybe they should take a little break somewhere bright and warm before he went on to his next assignment. Vic would probably understand, given the circumstances.

Lara sat in her playpen, clutching Baa-Baa and watching Mommy make dinner.

"Mommy?"

Mommy didn't turn around, didn't answer. "Mommy?"

Why didn't Mommy answer?

Lara stood up, Baa-Baa in one hand, and grabbed the rim of the playpen.

"*Mommy?*"

Mommy turned around. She looked mad. Lara stepped back, accidentally dropping Baa-Baa over the side of the playpen. She shrieked and started to cry.

"Gimme Baa-Baa!"

Mommy turned back around, grabbed something, then came at Lara with something shiny and sharp in her hand. She picked her up, fast and mean, and dropped her down on the floor in the corner. The floor was so hard, it knocked all the air right out of her mouth.

Mommy held her down with one arm, then raised up the shiny-sharp thing.

Mommy looked mad. Why was she so mad?

Lara's piercing scream jolted Kyle to his feet. He ran into the kitchen, stopping short as he took in the sight.

Gretchen crouched in the corner, where she'd pinned Lara's tiny body against the wall with her left arm across the child's chest and arms. Lara howled in terror and stared up, wide-eyed, at the butcher knife Gretchen held aloft in her right hand.

"No!" Kyle burst forward, but too late.

Gretchen ignored him and swung her arm down before he could stop her. Lara screamed even louder as the knife sliced into her tiny shoulder. Blood welled up, soaking her pink-and-white-dotted T-shirt and dripping onto the tile floor beside her. She squirmed frantically, but could not free herself. Gretchen again raised the bloody knife high as she adjusted her grip on the shrieking, blood-slippery child.

Before she could strike again, Kyle grabbed Gretchen's right wrist with one hand and her shoulder with the other. He yanked her back, away from Lara. She kicked and screamed and struggled to free herself from his grip as he dragged her across the tiles to the opposite end of the kitchen.

He twisted her wrist, hard. "Drop it!"

She screamed and fought him, her face red, her eyes wild and devoid of recognition. She displayed a shocking amount of strength despite her weakened condition. Kyle shoved her down onto her back and straddled her. She swiped at him with the knife until he finally twisted her wrist hard enough that she released it. He pinned her arm down with a knee, grabbed the knife, and tossed it up and away into the sink.

He stole a quick glance at Lara. She lay slumped in the corner, blood pooling around her across the flesh-colored tiles. Her screams had weakened to whimpers and her face had turned a deathly marble-white. She couldn't withstand that rate of blood loss for long, but Kyle didn't dare let go of Gretchen, or she'd try to kill them both.

He shouted into her face, "What is the matter with you?"

Gretchen kept screaming and struggling like a woman possessed. She whipped her head back and forth, trying to get close enough to bite his arm. She needed sedation, but he had nothing to give her, and no spare hands to do it with. He could only hope she'd tire before he did, but she showed no signs of it. If only he could call for an ambulance, but his cell was in the other room.

Lara looked worse each time he had a chance to glance in her direction. Her face had gone slack as she lay in a puddle of blood, silent and still now. He couldn't even tell if she was still alive. Fear, screaming, and struggle consumed Kyle for several minutes more, until he heard the sirens. Someone must have called 911 because of all the screaming. It sounded like murder.

Moments later, a knock sounded on the door. "Police! Open up!"

"In the kitchen—can't come to the door!"

The front door crashed open and two uniformed policemen rushed into the kitchen, guns drawn. One of them kept his gun trained on Kyle and Gretchen, while the other holstered his gun, then quickly went over to Lara. He checked her pulse.

"She's still alive! I'll radio the ambulance." He scooped up her limp body and dashed into the living room.

"What's going on?" The remaining policeman shouted over Gretchen's screaming and stood, legs set, ready to fire if need be.

"My wife. She went ..." Kyle suddenly realized the significance of Gretchen's behavior, and he felt sick. The antibiotics had been too late. Still pinning her to the floor, he bowed his head, the strength draining from him, as Gretchen continued to scream and struggle, oblivious to everything around her.

"What, sir? What's going on? Is she on drugs?"

"No. She ... she's having a sort of breakdown. She became violent." He sobbed. "She stabbed Lara before I could stop her."

Keeping his eyes trained on Gretchen, the officer turned his head partway toward the kitchen doorway. "Dennis, come back in here and help me soon as you can." He shifted his stance. "All right, we're going to restrain her. I need you to let go and step away as we get her under control."

"Okay." He didn't know how much longer he could hold her anyway.

Dennis entered the kitchen and shouted to be heard. "She's unconscious and still bleeding through the compress, but I got it to slow some. I found her crib and put her in there for now."

"Good. The wife's having some kind of psych episode. Get the riot cuffs on her, so he can step away and we can get some control here. Careful, Dennis." He aimed his gun directly at Gretchen's head.

"Got it." Dennis reached for the plastic zip cuffs on his service belt. He approached Gretchen's writhing body and, after several failed attempts, managed to cuff her wrists.

Kyle eased off her and tried to push himself up. His knees buckled and he crumpled to the floor, watching the horrifying scene play out in front of him. Cuffed and furious, Gretchen started kicking in all directions, screaming until her voice began to fray. Dennis dropped to the floor and pinned her legs with his body as he zip-cuffed her ankles. She lay there writhing and screaming, but no longer able to hurt herself or anyone else.

The first officer holstered his gun. "I'll go out and meet the ambulance."

Shaking, Kyle struggled up onto one of the kitchen chairs. He wanted to cover his ears, to block out Gretchen's screaming, but he was too weary even for that. He felt like he was somehow to blame, so he just let her increasingly hoarse cries batter him.

"Sir, they'll be right up to take care of them. There's no point in you staying in here right now." The second officer touched Kyle's shoulder and gazed down at him with an empathetic look on his face. "Why don't we leave them alone to do their job?"

"Sure, okay."

"Get your jacket first. It's beginning to snow."

"Oh, right. Thanks." Kyle grabbed his jacket from the closet by the door, then hung his head and followed the officer out as Gretchen screamed on.

They passed the paramedics in the hall as they headed for the elevator. Sitting inside the patrol car, Kyle did his best to answer the officer's questions as the paramedics worked on Gretchen and Lara upstairs, but he barely registered what they were asking him.

"Thank you, sir. That'll be all."

They both waited in the police car in awkward silence as a light snow fell around them. A short while later, the first officer emerged and held the hotel door open. The paramedics came out, each pushing a gurney. Kyle was relieved to see Gretchen lying still beneath her blanket. They must have sedated her.

The first officer returned to the patrol car and opened the door. "Sir, they're about ready to go. We can escort you to the hospital, if you'd like."

"Thanks, I'd appreciate that." Kyle got out, pulled his car around behind the ambulance and waited, engine idling. Snowflakes danced and winked in the hotel lights as they slid Gretchen and Lara into the waiting ambulance.

The paramedics closed the ambulance's back door with a loud slam—the sound of lives changing forever.

CHAPTER 62

Ted Warner stared, mesmerized, at the newsfeed on his office computer. Streaming video showed yet another incident in progress, this time a mass shooting at an oil refinery in Texas. Twenty people dead and counting, as well as an explosion that had flattened about a third of the plant and set off a massive fire that threatened a low-income neighborhood nearby.

One more problem to solve: the violence stemming from the valine problem. He had a plan worked out, but knew it would be—to say the least—controversial. Not to mention expensive. But it didn't matter. He had authority to do whatever needed to be done to protect the Homeland from terrorists. And as far as he was concerned, *terrorist* was a broad term indeed.

First things first. It was all well and good to say *B. metasonis* occurred in forty-seven percent of the population, but who were those people and where were they? Step one would be to identify the enemy of the Homeland: anyone harboring that bacteria.

So he declared a Homeland Security Emergency, which gave him the power to commandeer resources as he wished. Using that power, he ordered local police in all jurisdictions to go out and collect samples from everyone. Fortunately, the process didn't require any complicated training. Local labs had been instructed to process the samples as they were collected. It was the most efficient way to cover the entire Homeland that he could come up with.

Then the identity and personal information of those individuals testing positive would be forwarded to his department for further action.

He frowned at his computer screen. He hated how the liberal media made such a big deal of something so simple and so necessary. After all, it was for the Homeland's own good. Now they were airing video of a young family cowering in terror at their front door as the police showed up with their test kits.

Well, anyone who tested positive did have a lot to worry about. Those who didn't had nothing at all to fear and could go about their business.

He'd already tested negative for the bacteria. Good thing. He had a lot of work ahead of him to prepare for the elimination phase. But first, it would take several weeks of intense activity to obtain the complete list of carriers.

Ted sat back and considered exactly what to do about those carriers once he had the list. Always best to start planning early.

CHAPTER 63

Stu Walters fidgeted with his notepad as he waited for everyone to take their seat at the executive conference table. Early December already. Animal-protein- and soy-based foods had been banned for several months now and malnutrition had become widespread, especially among the more vulnerable populations. Time was ticking, and he worried that another BigAg company might get the jump on Cornucopia. And that he could not have.

"All right, let's get right to it. How close are we with the lab-raised meat?"

Ken Barnes, head of product development, cleared his throat and avoided eye contact. "We've made progress, Stu. Just not as much as we'd like."

"How so?"

"Well, we're ready to start producing Version 1.0, but 2.0 is still … presenting some challenges."

"Explain."

"We can produce the flat-sheet form of the product in volume now, and it tests clean. The amino acids are all in the proper form, no valine issues. It's reasonably palatable, but of course, because it comes in sheets, it can't deliver the experience of biting into a steak. Not yet."

"What's the holdup?"

"Trouble with the tissue scaffolding design. That's critical to producing something that actually looks like a steak and has integrated marbling."

Eric Regan, head of marketing, scowled as he made a note, then looked up. "Under normal circumstances—*normal* being where there were competing alternatives—this would be a product-killer. But I think my team can design a campaign that would work." He shrugged. "You want beef these days, you take what you can get."

Ken ran a hand through his hair. "And we're still working hard on the scaffolding. Don't get me wrong. We'll get there, but not as soon as I'd hoped."

Stu nodded. He had no doubt they were working on it as fast as they could. But it would all be for nothing if the competition leapfrogged them, so he had to keep up the pressure. "All right, keep me posted. What's the product name going to be?"

"SmartBeef. We want to make sure the consumer doesn't get the idea it's fake or substitute beef. It *is* real. And it's *smart* for them to eat it. They'll get a new source of complete protein that is certified safe to eat." Eric smiled.

Stu leaned back in his chair and considered the name for a moment. "I like it. I like it a lot. Let's go with that. Get it into production ASAP. We've got to get out there *first*—and our bottom line could use the boost. The losses in the soybean division have been staggering."

He adjourned the meeting and headed back to his office. Maybe the timing would work in their favor after all. Consumers would be so desperate for beef by now they'd snap this stuff up while they worked out the kinks in Version 2.0.

Hell, a beef dinner in about any form was starting to sound good about now.

CHAPTER 64

"Thanks for watching her. I know you're all very busy here."

"No problem, Dr. Sommers. She's such a sweet little girl. We enjoy having her around." A look of weary sadness crossed the nurse's face. "She brightens things up around here." She squatted down to Lara's eye level and smiled. "Come on, honey. Let's go to the playroom for a while." She picked her up, taking care not to bump her injured shoulder.

"'Bye, Daddy!" Lara waved her good arm and flashed a smile over the nurse's shoulder.

"'Bye, Lara. Be a good girl, okay?" He waved back.

Kyle stifled a yawn as he watched them head down the hall toward the children's room. The horror of what had happened was still every bit as potent for him as it was that night a couple of weeks ago. He spent his days dealing with the consequences of the attack, both practical and emotional, and sleep had been hard to come by. Every single night, as soon as he fell asleep, he relived the night of the attack in vivid detail and woke up drenched in sweat. He doubted he'd ever have peaceful dreams again. How could he, when his family and all sense of normalcy had been ripped apart?

Gretchen was admitted to Lakeside the night of the incident, like any other violent inmate, to await her turn through the legal process. And a long wait it would likely be, given the number of inmates already ahead of her, and the confusion in the courts. Judges were struggling with how to fairly assess guilt, given the physical basis for the violence.

Lara had spent several days in the ICU, and to the end of his days, he'd never forget how fragile she'd looked lying in that hospital bed, hooked up to IVs and monitors. So pale and weak. She'd lost a lot of blood in the attack and they'd had to give her several units of blood that night to stabilize her. Fortunately, she'd avoided any major physical damage. She was recovering well, considering.

She was full of questions every single day, questions that tore at him. Over and over she asked when would Mommy be coming home, where was Mommy—and why did Mommy want to hurt her? Of course, he had no words to explain any of that to a three-year-old child. So he did his best to duck her questions and hide his pain, at least for now.

He sighed, turned, and proceeded down the hall to where Gretchen awaited him. And it took every ounce of determination inside him to make that walk again, knowing what he would see and knowing what she had done.

Kyle reached the door to her ward, clenched his jaw, and forced himself to go inside. The sight sickened him as it did every time he'd come to see her: bed after bed arranged in double rows along each side of the long, harshly lit room. Each of the beds occupied—and equipped with restraints.

After the shooting a couple of months ago, the hospital made significant changes to protocol. The violent offenders were now fully segregated from the mental health patients. The rent-a-cops had been replaced by mandatory restraints and potent drugs to make the violent residents easier and safer for the limited staff to manage. Only staff that had tested negative for *B. metasonis* were allowed to report to work. The rest had been placed on paid leave for the time being.

The changes had somewhat stabilized the atmosphere at Lakeside, but the sheer number of new admissions continued to grow as time went on and more succumbed to the brain changes stemming from the malicious interaction of the malformed valine and *B. metasonis*. But despite the number of residents, an eerie silence hung over the ward.

He kept walking, passing bed after bed with some ruined, violent soul lying there, drugged and restrained like an animal. He averted his eyes, saving what strength he had for facing the sight of his Gretchen.

Kyle arrived at her bed and his vision blurred with hot, unshed tears as he gazed down. She lay there, her wrists and ankles peeking out from under the covers, tethered to thick metal bars with ugly, brown-padded-leather straps. Her deep blue eyes, once brilliant and lively, lay open and empty, sunken in darkened pools. She didn't even notice him there, she was so thoroughly drugged. She looked as if she might as well be dead.

And that was the hell of it. He knew the changes to her brain were permanent, irreversible. She could not be rehabilitated, and so would likely be committed here for the rest of her life.

Realistically, what else *could* be done with her? He'd seen firsthand what she was capable of. No matter what he did, no matter how much time passed, he would never be able to erase his mental image of her plunging that knife into Lara. He had no doubt whatsoever that if he hadn't intervened when he had, she would have killed Lara. No doubt at all. And she'd likely have turned the knife on him next. He feared her for it, but he couldn't hate her for it. Her brain had been altered. It wasn't really Gretchen who held the knife that night. It wasn't her fault, but the fact remained that she could never be trusted again.

He stood beside her bed, staring down at the antiseptic white linoleum floor. No, there was no other choice than to institutionalize her. It might be a little better if it were a private institution with fewer patients to tend to. Maybe. Or maybe it wouldn't matter to her, only to him.

In light of the situation, he'd asked for a leave of absence. Vic had been generous in granting him the time he needed, but added that when he returned, he wanted to present him with some form of recognition for his excellent work in unearthing the problem.

Nothing could be further from what Kyle wanted now. He wished to God he'd never even come here, never had anything to do with the investigation. He knew he didn't bring this onto Gretchen. But still, he harbored a form of guilt about it even though he knew it wasn't rational.

Kyle glanced out the grimy window at the end of the ward. Snow fell outside. It was nearly Christmas. He crumpled to the floor beside Gretchen's bed, put his face in his hands, and sobbed.

CHAPTER 65

Les Anderson lounged in his living room in the middle of the afternoon, something he hadn't had time to do in as long as he could remember. Demand for his services had disappeared nearly overnight, save for the occasional call to treat a household pet. Something had to give. He'd been a vet his entire adult life, and didn't know what else he could do—or would even want to do—for a living.

He pushed aside those thoughts for the moment and clicked on the television, for lack of anything better to do. Most of the time these days he wondered at the point of even watching the news at all. Every report was a tragic déjà vu of protests, panic, lost jobs, and food shortages. People killing wild game—and each other. And now, sure as shit, malnutrition had become rampant.

People were starting to die.

First it was the vulnerable ones. The old, the ones with chronic conditions. Pregnant women were miscarrying at a shocking rate. Those few who did make it to term generally didn't survive childbirth. Newborn deaths were skyrocketing. It was as if third-world malnutrition had come to the United States. Children were dying now, too, their little bellies bulging beneath their shirts.

Les clicked off the TV and flung the remote across the room. It shattered against the wall with a satisfying crash. He covered his face with his hands, letting the hot tears flow as he sobbed, his entire body shuddering with overwhelming grief. All his life, he'd been devoted to treating farm animals. His good care enabled the farmers to put nutritious, quality food on people's tables. Now those animals had become poison, and people were dying because of it.

He wondered if there was any future left, or if this was the food chain's version of Armageddon.

CHAPTER 66

Stu Walters glanced at the report in his hand, then at Ken Barnes, whom he'd called into his office for an emergency meeting along with Eric Regan. "SmartBeef is too expensive. Sales are crap."

Ken stared down at the papers in his lap. "Well, we're still working out some kinks in the production process. Normal stuff for a new product, nothing unusual. I agree, it's pricey per pound, but our margin isn't much right now. I'm hoping when we smooth out our production lines that we can lower the price and still make money on it."

"I think we need to lower the price *now*, even if that would make it a loss leader. We've got to get more people to at least try it and see it's the best there is on the market. I've tried it myself. It tastes good, but the form of it is, frankly, off-putting. We need to overcome that and build product loyalty in the near term."

Ken nodded. "Understood. By the way, we've nearly solved the scaffolding problem on the 2.0 version. Might be several months before we're ready to start producing it, but at least we're finally about through that roadblock. It's been a real bear."

"That's good news. The 2.0 version'll be a great product, but I suspect it will be substantially more expensive to produce, at least in the near term. We need to round out our offerings with a second-tier product that doesn't try so hard."

"What do you mean?" Ken raised an eyebrow.

"The nonprescription version of our pharmaceutical liquid diet. We talked about it a couple of months ago."

"Oh, right. I remember we brainstormed it, but SmartBeef took priority in the meantime."

"Conditions are ripe for consumers to accept this sort of product now. We could capture those who can't afford or won't accept SmartBeef, as well as the vegetarians who've lost their soy-based dietary protein sources."

Eric gazed up at the ceiling as he spoke. "A portable, ultra-convenient way to get your day's nutrition. A product that fits right into people's busy, mobile lives." He scribbled a few notes. "I'll get the campaign ready right away."

Ken brightened. "We can have it in production and distribution well before SmartBeef 2.0."

"Then make it so. Get it done and out there as fast as you can, of course making sure to test it for safety."

CHAPTER 67

Jeff McClain seated himself at his dining room table, folded his arms, and gazed at his dinner plate. He didn't like what he saw there, but he'd run out of choices. His dealer had disappeared on him weeks ago, and he'd been unable to find a real steak anywhere ever since.

He took a sip of his Merlot and considered the irony of his situation. Here he was on the outskirts of Kansas City, arguably the meat capital of the United States—at least it used to be. And he'd finally had to resort to purchasing beef that had been grown in a lab. He wondered how good—or bad—it would be.

He glanced over toward the glass sliders, at the snow falling on the cedar deck beneath the porch lights. Nearly Christmastime. He thought back to memorable holiday meals with his extended family, back when they were still around. Every year, they'd all get together and share a huge, juicy prime rib roast with all the trimmings. Those were the days. His relatives had all since passed away, and he'd never married. Such was life. So he took his pleasures in good food, especially a good cut of beef. Now even that had been taken away from him.

Jeff sighed and stared down at his plate, at the flat plank of lab-produced beef that lay there. It looked more like a wide piece of jerky than anything else. If that. He'd carefully sautéed it in a little olive oil and garlic, along with some black pepper. It was so thin, he feared a high heat would toughen it right into shoe leather. There it sat, next to a baked potato. A baked potato dotted with margarine, of course, since real butter was banned these days.

He cut a piece of the meat, stared at it on his fork for a

moment, then put it in his mouth. He chewed cautiously, not sure of what to expect, though for what the stuff cost per pound, it ought to be damned good. He swallowed, then tried another piece.

After a few bites, he decided it was a thin impersonation of the real thing. Yeah, Cornucopia said it was real beef, from actual beef tissue, and that may be. But it lacked the complex flavor and texture he loved and missed so much. Maybe for someone who'd never enjoyed a good cut of fresh beef, it would be satisfying. For him, it was more of a tease, making him wish he had a steak. One produced the old-fashioned way.

At least SmartBeef didn't contain the problem protein that had started all the trouble. He never was sure about the beef his dealer had sold him. He'd claimed it had never been fed soy, but there was no way to confirm that. And if he'd ever found out the dealer had been lying, he couldn't exactly go to the cops about it or sue him.

Even if it wasn't as satisfying as a normal steak, it would be good to get some proper protein and iron again. He'd been feeling somewhat weak and lethargic lately from trying to get his protein from beans, rice, and nuts.

He'd never been able to stomach fish.

CHAPTER 68

Les Anderson switched on his wipers to clear the snow and slush from his truck's windshield before it iced over. He was out driving in moderate, mid-December snow—more for old time's sake than for any real reason. He had no house calls to make, no one to visit, no errands to run. It depressed him, having nothing to do. Given the winter gloom outside, he could either sit in semidarkness in his house, or he could turn on all the lights to dispel it. But he knew that wouldn't work.

So he'd decided to get out in the truck and take a drive, despite the weather, just to get himself moving and to get some fresh air, frigid though it might be. He pulled over near the edge of Marty Janssen's place, killed the engine, and got out.

Gloved hands in pockets and the hood of his down jacket snugged around his face to keep out the cold and wet, he walked slowly along the fence line, his boots crunching in the snow, and gazed at Marty's spread. A chill—unrelated to the weather—went through him as he took in the view.

Empty. So damned empty. Where normally the snowy pasture would be dotted with cattle, there lay an expanse of clean, unbroken whiteness. If he didn't know better, he'd think Marty had pulled up stakes and left the place, livestock and all. But he knew he was there, doing his best to survive by starting up that fish-breeding operation out back. He shook his head. So much had changed in a few months. At least Marty and Paul were working on a Plan B. All the rest of his clients were hunkered down for the winter, witnessing the certain deaths of their livelihoods.

He didn't know which was worse: to lie down and accept

what had happened, or to kill yourself trying something risky to change it. Marty and Paul were taking a shot, for sure, but they might well be working their asses off to wind up the same as their neighbors in the end. He hoped they made it—for their sakes, and especially for Susan's—but raising fish up here seemed crazy to him.

Les stopped, leaned over, and rested his arms on the wood fence. Sitting alone in his house, he could almost convince himself that something would change soon, that things would return to normal and he could continue with his veterinary practice. But here, out in the field where things were real, he could see that wasn't true. There was nothing left for him anymore, just as there was nothing left for any of his clients.

He'd become obsolete, and he didn't have the energy or desire to make something new of himself at his age. He pursed his lips and frowned, then took one last look at Marty's pasture and got back in his truck. He started it, wipered the snow off the windshield, and pulled back onto the road with no particular destination in mind.

CHAPTER 69

Long after everyone else had gone home for the night, Ted Warner sat in his office, staring at his computer screen with bleary eyes as he scrolled through the threat data compiled so far. He had assistants organizing the lab results as they came in and entering them into a single database for his use. For each individual tested, it contained: name, ID number, full address, age, sex, whether the individual harbored *B. metasonis*, and whether the individual was already detained by law enforcement. He could filter and sort the data as he wished.

The overall percentage of positives was in line with what he expected, about forty-seven percent. There was nothing special about the geographic distribution, except that families living together tended to all harbor the specific strain of bacteria.

The testing phase would be complete soon, and he needed to be ready to act on the results. He considered the possibilities. Those who tested negative were in the clear—at least for now. It might be wise to retest that part of the population in the future, to see if they somehow acquired the bacteria later on. But that was a question for another day.

For those who tested positive—and weren't already under some form of detention—what to do? Ted sat back in his chair and rubbed his eyes as he worked through the problem. Was there any time gap to exploit between the consumption of the defective valine and the eventual effects on the brain? If there was, then maybe the mandatory administration of antibiotics to kill the *metasonis* would suffice to break the chain. If not, then he'd have to more aggressive in his approach. Much more aggressive.

And if no one knew the answer with certainty, then he'd be better off going all out to eradicate the problem. The Homeland could not continue to suffer from the violence that plagued it. It wasn't his job to be popular; it was his job to keep the Homeland safe. At any cost.

CHAPTER 70

Kyle pulled his rented Camry into Lakeside's parking lot and idled for a few minutes with the heater blasting. Fortunately, he'd found a sympathetic neighbor at the extended-stay place to watch Lara when he went to visit Gretchen each day. It wasn't the ideal situation, but it was better than dragging her to the hospital and having an already overworked nurse take time away from all those patients to watch her.

For that matter, nothing whatsoever about their situation was ideal at the moment, and he had no idea what to do about that. He spent his days mired in it, helpless to make things better, let alone right. It tore at his heart every time Lara looked up at him with those pleading eyes and asked about her mommy—and why did Mommy get so mad at her that she had to hurt her? He wondered how long she would swallow the story that Mommy just needed a little rest.

The painful routine had gone on for a little more than a month now, with no end in sight. Eventually, he'd have to think of something more long-term. This wasn't their home, and they couldn't live in this suspended animation indefinitely. If Gretchen had to remain institutionalized the rest of her life, they should at least relocate either her or themselves to regain some semblance of stability. Vic had been generous about granting him leave, but that couldn't last forever and there would be bills to pay. He'd have to return to work at some point, and now he wasn't even sure he wanted to return to the EIS.

He wiped the condensation off the inside of the windshield with his mittened hand and glanced up. The mid-January snow had stopped for now, but the gunmetal gray sky hinted at more to come. He sighed, shut off the engine and prepared himself to go in there and visit Gretchen.

If you could call it visiting, that is. Like all the other violent residents, they had her so heavily drugged she barely seemed alive, let alone conscious of his presence. He wondered if Gretchen would remember what she'd done to Lara if she were less medicated. Maybe it was better for her to be shielded from that memory.

As he kicked the snow from his boots and entered the hospital, he saw several nurses and orderlies clustered farther down the hall. He stopped at the nurses' station and asked the duty nurse about the commotion.

"Well, since you're from the EIS, I suppose it's okay to tell you. In fact, you *should* be told, now that I think of it."

"Tell me what?"

"The strangest thing. The ones who're here because the jails filled up have been dying. It started with the ones who came here first. Then the ones who came in the next wave. It seems related to the time since the onset of their violent symptoms."

Kyle took a sharp breath as the implications struck him. The first wave had come in about six months ago. Was it possible that the condition was terminal? And if so, what did that mean for Gretchen? His throat tightened at the thought.

"Have they been performing autopsies?"

"Yes, though they're getting a little backed up now. Dr. Kaiser could tell you what they've found so far. He's probably downstairs in the morgue. I could let him know you need to speak with him."

"Yes, please do. I'd like to have a word with him after I visit my wife."

"I'll tell him, Dr. Sommers."

"Thanks." Kyle turned and headed toward Gretchen's ward, his mind reeling. Was there any way to prevent the deaths? And would there be any point in it? If the brain change was permanent and those affected couldn't be rehabilitated, was there really anything humane to be done for them?

But Gretchen …

He stepped into her ward and averted his eyes from the

other beds as he approached hers. He stopped at the foot of her
bed and gazed at her. No change. None whatsoever. She still
looked like she wasn't even there. Of course, the drugs had a lot
to do with that, but now that her brain was changed, who was
she? Was she even Gretchen anymore?

Kyle moved to the head of her bed. He took her cool, soft
hand in his, wincing at the sight of the vile leather restraint that
tethered her wrist. He squeezed her limp hand. No response.
Her glazed eyes stared straight up at the ceiling.

He leaned down close to her and spoke softly near her ear.
"Gretchen … Gretchen, do you hear me?" He straightened up
again and stared down at her blank, drawn face. She wasn't
even getting a decent diet in this place. Good protein sources
inexpensive enough for institutional use remained unattainable.

He took a deep breath and sighed. She didn't even know he
was there. He might as well go see Dr. Kaiser and find out what
was going on. He reached down and gently touched her cheek.

Her eyes suddenly widened and she turned to him, an
expression of pure hate on her face. She snarled and tried to
bite him, growling and snapping like some vicious, rabid beast.
He jumped back, startled and terrified, nearly tripping in his
haste. She fought her restraints and screamed. Patients around
her reacted to the uproar in kind, shrieking and struggling in
their beds.

He clapped his hands to his ears and staggered out of the
ward to go alert the nurse.

Kyle parked himself in a stiff vinyl chair in the visitors' lounge,
elbows on knees and a paper cup of cold water in his hands.
He took a sip now and then, more for something to do than
anything else. The lounge was empty except for him, and he
was grateful for the solitude. Gretchen's episode reawakened his
memory of that horrible night she tried to kill Lara—that look in
her eye, that evil determination she had. He now believed that
the last time he saw her before that attack was the last time he
would ever again see the Gretchen he'd known, loved, and had
married.

The door to the visitors' lounge swung open. An older

man in green scrubs stepped in and glanced toward him. "Dr. Sommers, I presume?"

He set his cup on the table beside his chair, then stood. "Yes, that's me."

The other man approached him and held out his hand. "I'm Dr. Kaiser. I understand you wanted to speak with me."

"Yes. Yes, I did." Kyle shook his hand, then sat back down.

Dr. Kaiser pulled up a chair, lowered himself into it as if he carried a hundred-pound weight on his back, and let out a long, weary breath. "Looks like this is as good a place as any. We don't get many visitors here anymore." He raised an eyebrow and smiled. "I understand you're the EIS investigator who figured this all out."

"Yes, I am." Kyle didn't feel like enduring a round of congratulations for his work, so he moved on quickly. "I understand there've been fatalities—specifically among those in the first wave of admissions. Well, not the usual admissions, but the ones they housed here because of the lack of jail space."

Dr. Kaiser rubbed his temples as if he had a headache. "That's right. When I look at their admission dates, it's almost like a switch went off. Those who began exhibiting their violent symptoms right about six months ago, they're the ones dying now. The correlation is quite consistent."

"What's the cause of death?"

"To be honest, I've gotten behind because of the volume, so I haven't examined them all yet. But the ones I have autopsied all show the same pathology." He paused and stared at the floor. "I've never seen anything like it. In each of them, without exception, the amygdala has hypertrophied—grown to the extent that it created massive intracranial pressure and eventually crushed the rest of the brain."

"How could this happen? It wouldn't be an overnight process."

"No, six months isn't exactly overnight, but it does indicate rather rapid growth of that portion of the brain. The heavy meds they keep those patients on likely masked any symptoms, like the intense headaches that would've undoubtedly accompanied that kind of growth. An unexpected mercy, I'd say."

"So do you think ..." Kyle swallowed, then forced himself to choke out the next words. "Do you think anything can be done proactively for the others?"

Dr. Kaiser sighed and shook his head. "No. I don't even see what *could* be done. The tissue wasn't cancerous—not that brain cancer is a cinch to treat. So chemo wouldn't have worked. It simply grew and took over. Cancer-like in that way, but without the abnormal cells associated with cancer. Just totally normal cells, growing and multiplying at an incredibly rapid rate. No, I don't think there is anything that can be done to stop the process."

Kyle picked up his cup and took a sip of water, then set the cup back down before speaking again. "So, you expect to see more of this."

"If it keeps to the pattern, I expect I'll be able to predict it by looking at admit dates. I'm sorry I didn't get this information out to EIS or you before. I got hit with such a wave of it, then only recently finished enough posts to see the pattern."

"I'm actually on leave right now, but I'll make sure the information gets to the right place."

"Oh, I thought you came here to investigate the deaths." Dr. Kaiser wore a puzzled look.

Kyle hesitated, then stared down at the linoleum floor, white and cold as death. "I'm here visiting my wife. She was admitted last month." He looked back up, straight into Dr. Kaiser's eyes. "So I guess she has about five months left."

CHAPTER 71

Vic Rayburn hesitated before knocking. He didn't like it one bit when the Department of Homeland Security felt it necessary to stick its nose in CDC business. He accepted that programs like forced quarantine were sometimes justified as a last resort, but DHS seemed far more willing to suspend civil liberties than he thought was appropriate.

His discomfort had risen to an all-time high since Ted Warner took over as chief of DHS. The man was simply incapable of taking individual rights into consideration. And now he wanted to discuss the valine problem again. Vic had been alarmed enough when Ted had mandated testing the entire population for *B. metasonis*. He dreaded what today's conversation might entail.

He raised his hand and knocked.

"Come in."

Vic let himself in and took a seat without offering to shake hands. He had to admit national security had been disrupted by the wave of violence. Now that they knew the cause, and that it had a physical mechanism, Ted would undoubtedly want to take some over-the-top action. Vic was afraid to hear what Ted had in mind.

"First, I want to say, nice work by your department, Vic. Really impressive. You've got some sharp people, or we'd still be fighting the symptoms, rather than the root of the problem."

Vic bristled at Ted's disingenuous smile. "Thanks. Got a great crop of investigators in the program this year."

The smile disappeared as quickly as it had materialized, leaving a cold, ruthless look in its wake. "Well, I know you're a busy man, so I'll get right to the point." Ted waved his hand toward his PC. "When we finish processing the results, we'll have a database of all individuals who harbor *metasonis*. I need to ask you a few questions so I can plan what to do next."

"Yeah." Vic could feel his jaw clench.

Ted rubbed his palms together. "So, once someone who harbors *metasonis* has been exposed to the defective valine, is there any question that they'll become violent at some point?"

Vic shifted in his chair. "We don't know for sure. We do know that once violence is exhibited, it isn't reversible. But it's impossible to do random, controlled testing under the circumstances. The brain changes might be preventable if the bacteria were eliminated before they responded to the defective valine. But we don't know if that's possible, and if it is, how long that window might be."

Ted scowled as he absorbed the information. "What happens once an individual becomes violent—other than the obvious? What happens after that point? Presumably anyone who's already exhibited violence has been taken into custody, right?"

"That's correct. Depending on local jail capacity, many of these individuals have been transferred to mental institutions, for both space and care considerations. We're getting reports now that this condition runs a certain predictable course. After about six months from the onset of violent symptoms, death results from hypertrophy of the amygdala."

"What?"

Vic sighed. "One portion of the brain grows so fast, it crushes the rest of the brain inside the skull."

Ted's eyes lit up. "You mean it's self-limiting? They die after six months?"

Vic wanted to slap the gleeful look off Ted's face. "Apparently so. And because of the nature of the growth, there appears to be no treatment available. It's a death sentence for these people."

Ted leaned back in his chair, gazed up at the ceiling, and gnawed on the end of his pen. "Well, that solves part of the problem quite nicely. Self-limiting, and the deaths will also reopen storage space for those who'll become violent later on. I wish we had better information about any window of time to eliminate the bacteria before the brain changes are triggered." He dropped his pen on his desk with an air of finality. "We'll have to make do with what we have."

Ted's sanguine tone made Vic uneasy. "What do you mean?"

"We'll have to head off whatever cases we can proactively. Is there an existing antibiotic that eliminates *metasonis*?"

"Well, yes."

Ted leaned forward and started making notes on a pad. "Good. Now. We'll be dealing with a lot of recipients, so we need compliance to be as simple as possible. Can it be administered in a single injection, as opposed to some multi-day pill regimen?"

"It can, but the pill regimen is preferred for a number of reasons. *Metasonis* is only sensitive to one antibiotic. Unfortunately, that antibiotic causes severe side effects in certain people, as well as fetal death in pregnant women. With the pill regimen, it's at least possible to stop treatment if problems arise. With the single injection, there's no turning back and any reaction would be swifter and far more severe."

Ted avoided eye contact as he made more notes and spoke in a matter-of-fact tone. "That's unfortunate, but we don't have the resources to monitor compliance. Not on this scale. We need to be able to administer, confirm, and chip each recipient on the spot. Bad enough we don't know if this will prevent a single case. But it sounds like it's the only proactive thing left that we can do."

"We don't know that it'll prevent any cases. It's not worth the risk to those who would have dangerous reactions to the drug."

Ted looked up, shook his head, and made a dismissive gesture with his hand. "That doesn't even make sense on its face. Vic, you have to understand, this is a compromise on my part. The alternative is to simply detain everyone who tested positive for *metasonis,* for as long as necessary. That would really be the ultimate way to protect the Homeland from those people, those … time bombs waiting to become violent."

"You'd really do that if you could, wouldn't you?"

Ted gave him a surprised look. "Of course I would. It offers perfect protection, given the nature of the problem. If I had the space capacity to do it, you can be sure I'd have already issued the order."

CHAPTER 72

Celia's breath caught when she heard the knock at her front door. It was the knock she'd been dreading. She held her six-year-old son Joey in her lap and instinctively tightened her arms around him. He'd been home from school for days, sick with some bug or another. He'd always been a sickly kid, allergic to everything.

She knew from the news stories that the police were going door to door to the homes of everyone who tested positive for that stomach bacteria that reacted with meats and other animal-protein products. Well, they'd taken those products off the shelves months ago. Why wasn't that enough?

The government was supposed to make sure that food was safe, so how this mess happened in the first place was beyond her. It was all she could do to take care of Joey by herself and try to hang on to her job. Day-to-day existence was a struggle as it was.

The knock sounded again, this time accompanied by an impatient, "Ms. Weldon, open up. We're here for Joey Weldon, to give him his medication."

Celia remained silent, trembling and holding her son close. Maybe if they thought she wasn't home, they'd go away.

"Mommy, what do the men want?"

"Shush. Keep quiet."

"We know you're home, and we have authority to come in by force if you make that necessary." The voice sounded tired but serious.

Her mouth dry, she shifted Joey off her lap and onto the couch, then rose slowly. "Stay there a minute, baby."

He looked up at her with tired, sunken eyes. "Okay, Mom."

If they came in by force, they'd wreck the door. And then she'd owe the landlord for the repair. There was no money for that—not for that *and* food. She was barely able to feed them both on her income as it was, especially with the prices of the more nutritious foods going through the roof.

She went to the front door and peered out the peephole. Two uniformed policemen stood on her front steps, accompanied by a man wearing a white coat. They'd scare Joey for sure.

One of the cops rapped at the door, hard this time. "*Now*, Ms. Weldon, or we come in."

Sighing, she unlocked the door and opened it slowly. They wasted no time coming in. The man in the white coat consulted a paper list in his hand.

"Joey Weldon, age six." He glanced toward the couch. "There he is." Then he walked right over to Joey before Celia could say or do anything.

She started toward her son, but one of the cops gripped her upper arm.

"Wait here, Ms. Weldon. You can be arrested for interfering. Matter of national security. We have orders."

She tried to pull away. "I don't care about your orders! He's not well today. Can't you come back when he's stronger?"

"No, ma'am. Too many homes to visit. We can't take the time to come back. This'll only take a minute."

Joey shrank back into the couch and screeched as the man in white approached him. "Mommy, I'm scared!"

The man turned and gave a slight nod of his head. The second cop swiftly went over and pinned Joey down.

"Don't hurt him!" Celia leapt forward to protect her little boy, but the first cop held her back. She struggled in his grip.

The man in white spoke in a calm, matter-of-fact tone. "This will only take a moment, I promise. One quick injection, and he'll get the antibiotic to eliminate the problem bacteria, and a tiny chip coded to prove he's received the injection. Very quick, very efficient."

"But he's allergic to a lot of stuff. How do we know he's not allergic to this?"

"There are no exemptions. National security." The man reached into a small zipped bag he'd been carrying and brought out an individually wrapped syringe. Joey struggled, screamed, and hyperventilated as the second cop held him firmly to the couch. The man pushed up Joey's T-shirt sleeve and quickly administered the shot. Then he nodded to the cop, who released the crying boy. He took a separate container from his bag, placed the used syringe in it, then stood to leave.

"That's it." He smiled and winked. "Told you it was quick."

The cop released Celia's arm. "Thank you, Ms. Weldon. Sorry to have disturbed you."

The two cops and the man in the white coat had just stepped out the front door when Joey began wheezing. Celia ran to him and held him in her arms. She didn't like how he was breathing.

"Wait! I think he's having a reaction!"

The first cop turned to her. "We're not trained to deal with that. I'll call 911 for you when I get out to the car. They should be here soon. Good-bye."

And with that, they left, shutting the door behind them. Celia rocked Joey gently as she waited for help to arrive—and as his breathing worsened.

She did not like the bluish tinge in his lips.

CHAPTER 73

Vic Rayburn slammed his office door shut, flung himself into his chair, and put his head in his hands. He wanted to vomit. On the one hand, he was relieved to see the crisis appeared to be over, or nearly so. And he remained proud of Kyle Sommers's work in uncovering the complex problem. But when he saw Ted Warner's face plastered up on the news as if he were some sort of hero, his stomach turned.

The violence was definitely waning to pre-crisis levels. But despite Warner's bragging, it would never be known how effective the forced antibiotic administration had been. Vic doubted it had done much, given what Kyle had told him about his own failed attempt to treat Gretchen.

On the other hand, the number of people who'd had serious reactions to the antibiotic or died, well, *that* could be measured. And it was too high a price. As he'd told Warner, if those with the bacteria were already doomed or likely so, the risk of mandatory antibiotic administration without any regard for allergies or preexisting physical conditions was absolutely unwarranted.

But it was too late now. The injections had been administered a couple of months ago. Whatever good they were going to do was done, and whatever harm was already done as well.

Meanwhile, Warner had instituted additional intrusive procedures to help safeguard the Homeland. Anyone arrested for a violent act was immediately cross-checked against the master list of those who'd tested positive for *metasonis*. Those on the list were immediately institutionalized for the rest of their roughly six-month lives without any judicial oversight whatsoever. Otherwise, it was presumed to be a case of good old-fashioned criminal behavior, and they were prosecuted accordingly.

The actions that DHS had been able to undertake worried him, both in terms of the scope of its resources and the lack of public resistance in the face of the threat. What would happen the next time some sort of epidemic hit the country? Would Warner be that much bolder and more aggressive in tackling it? Did that man have any limits at all—and would the public again simply acquiesce to whatever he did?

Vic went over to his office window and gazed down at the cherry blossoms that brightened D.C. this time of year. Would this world ever be the same?

CHAPTER 74

Marty made the mistake of gazing out at his pastures from his living room window. He usually welcomed the early spring, when the bright, fragile green of emerging grass took over, pushing aside the last bits of stubborn snow. But usually, the sight included cattle nursing early calves. Not so this year. He had no livestock, and likely wouldn't again for several years. He turned away from the window, unable to bear the emptiness.

He trudged through the living room, unable to decide what to do with himself. The fish operation took a lot less daily chore time than his cattle operation did. A shame he couldn't take advantage of it and relax and enjoy the view outside. He glanced at his watch. Lunchtime, and he was kind of hungry. He decided to give himself a change of scenery and take a little drive to that café in St. Joe.

A short while later, he pulled up in front of the café, leaned his head out the window, and drew a deep breath of the crisp spring air. So much had changed in the last few months as winter released its bitter hold. He felt sadness and hope at the same time.

Marty bought a newspaper from the dispenser in front of the café, stepped inside and took a seat by himself at the end of the counter, away from the rest of the diners. He wasn't in much of a mood to socialize today. He glanced around at the place as he snapped open his paper.

One of the remaining local farmers had bankrolled his daughter Julie in renting the café and reopening it after that vegetarian from the Cities passed away. He shook his head. He'd heard about what happened to her, to all the vegetarians who'd thought they could safely eat soy products. Same damned thing that'd happened to his cattle. Something went screwy with the way their bodies manufactured their tissue, leading to premature aging, then premature death.

He'd avoided the place when the vegetarian ran it, trying to convince longtime beef farmers and their ilk that a vegetarian diet was the way to go, and serving it up amid her frilly pastel decor. Crazy thing to try in these parts. As it turned out, she'd been partly right, though not for the right reasons, and not right enough. Poor kid. Now he felt bad for being one of the folks who'd pointedly avoided her café. No one deserved what she'd gone through.

"What'll you have today, Marty?" Julie smiled and held her notepad at the ready.

"Oh, burger and coffee would be fine, thanks. How's it going?"

She tipped her head toward the customers laughing and talking at their tables. "Not bad for just starting out."

"Well, that's great to hear."

Her expression turned serious. "Yeah, the better I do, the sooner I can pay Dad back." She averted her eyes for a moment. "He needs the money." She smiled again, a wide, bright smile on her pretty face. "Hey, I'll get that burger out to you right quickly." She turned and headed back into the kitchen.

Marty watched her go, dressed in her crisp, light blue, almost retro-looking diner uniform. She seemed to be a good kid. He hoped the café did well. Folks deserved some good news and progress toward recovery, after all that had happened. As he glanced down at his paper, he couldn't help but think about how much everything had changed since that young doctor had come to town and figured out what the problem was.

No one he knew had any livestock left now. All the animals had died off or been destroyed—beef, dairy, poultry, hogs, everything. Couldn't sell 'em, why pour good money after bad feeding 'em? The BigAg suppliers hadn't yet come up with safe soybean stock, so there would be no planting any soy this season. Corn was still a good choice. At least there was a market for it for ethanol production. Hopefully there wouldn't be drought conditions again this year to kill off even that hope.

As for his aquaculture venture with Paul, winter heating bills had pushed them way into the red, but fish prices were still quite good and they stood to make some of that up in the next few months. At least it was still in the realm of possibility.

Julie reappeared with his food. "Here you go, Marty. Enjoy. Let me know if you want anything else."

"Thanks, Julie."

She smiled and nodded, then hustled over to a table full of customers by the front window.

He gazed down at his lunch. Some burger. It came in a bun, came with fries and all the trimmings—except cheese, of course—but it looked like one of them sliders they used to serve in the big-city brewpubs. Just a couple of discs of flat meat grown in the lab. He picked it up and regarded it for a moment before taking a bite. It was the best you could get if you were in the mood for some beef. Might as well make the best of it.

It was sure better than that liquid crap they were trying to sell these days. Unimaginable, drinking your day's meals. But at least the stuff supposedly contained complete protein, and was affordable. Malnutrition-related deaths—especially of kids—had certainly dropped since it came out. So he guessed that was a good thing, anyway.

Marty wished like hell he could return to the old days, when food was fresh and natural and you could trust it. He shrugged and took another bite of his burger. No way to turn back the clock, only look forward and try to survive as best you could.

CHAPTER 75

Kyle pulled up beneath a large, shady maple tree in Lakeside's parking lot. The July heat and humidity already bore down, though it was only mid-morning. He left the engine running with the air conditioner blasting as he prepared himself yet again.

It had been nearly a year since he'd accepted the assignment, a year that had brought so much change, so much devastation. Little Lara had turned four now, and in the past few months had begun to accept the status quo. She only asked about her mommy a couple of times a week now, rather than multiple times a day. While it pained him to see her make that adjustment, he knew it was for the best under the circumstances.

He'd extended his leave of absence several times since Gretchen was admitted to Lakeside. Vic had begun to ask him about his intentions, whether he planned to return to the EIS program. But he hadn't pressed hard. He knew what Kyle was facing, knew an end would come in due course.

Kyle drew a final deep breath of the chill air jetting from the vents. The coolness helped to steady him, a little. Then he got out of the car and went inside.

He'd been a daily visitor for so long, the hospital staff merely gave him friendly, yet solemn, nods when he came in. That was fine with him. It was hard enough to return, day after day, knowing what he knew—and seeing Gretchen as she'd become. Fortunately, Nutrio, that liquid food substitute that came out a few months ago, was cheap enough to use even in institutional settings. So at least Gretchen no longer had that drawn, fragile look of malnutrition about her.

Just that look of constant sedation.

Kyle knew the heavy sedation was in reality a mercy, both for her and for him. She wouldn't feel the pain of the relentless brain hypertrophy that was undoubtedly underway within her skull. And he didn't have to witness that pain, as well as the inevitable degradation of her cognitive abilities as the process unfolded. He'd accepted months ago that he'd lost his real Gretchen just before she snapped and tried to kill Lara—and that he'd never, ever have her back again.

He made his way down the line of beds. The place was somewhat less crowded than it had been at the height of the crisis. He supposed that was a good thing, a sign that this whole horrible chapter would eventually come to an end and those left in its wake could begin to heal and move on in a new world of lab-produced foods.

Kyle drew close to Gretchen's bed and gazed down at her as he'd done so many times before. Something seemed different today. Something he couldn't quite put his finger on. A sort of tension hung in the air. He frowned and peered at her more closely. Same motionless body, same vacant stare up toward the ceiling. At least her eyes were less sunken now that she was being fed Nutrio.

He touched her hand, and her response startled him. Her hand closed around his and remained like that, warm and intimate. No thrashing, no violence. Just holding hands, like the most natural thing in the world. For a moment, he was transported back to happier days, before any of the horrors and tragedies of the past year. On an impulse, he leaned over and gently kissed her on the lips. He thought he felt the slightest response in return.

Still leaning close to her face, he looked into her eyes, wishing for some sign of recognition, of consciousness, no matter how brief. A cold bolt shot through his stomach.

Her eyes were dilating, the pupils overtaking the deep blue of her irises like a fast-spreading malignancy. Before the dilation's significance hit him, full-body, uncontrollable spasms racked her. Sweat broke out on her forehead and white foam dribbled from the corners of her mouth. Her head whipped back and forth as she struggled against her restraints. She clenched her teeth so tightly, he heard several of them crack as inhuman, guttural sounds burst from her.

Kyle slammed the call button by her bed and stumbled backward. There was no safe way to try to hold her down or stop her. She needed an anticonvulsant. Then as suddenly as it began, her seizure ended. He bent close, ready to spring back out of the way if she started again.

Gretchen lay absolutely motionless, her pupils fixed and dilated. He placed a finger along her carotid. No pulse. He gently laid his hand on her sternum. No breath.

A nurse and an orderly rushed up to the bed. He shook his head. They nodded and, without a word, left him alone.

Kyle went around the bed, unfastening each of the leather restraints. At least Gretchen could have that much dignity now. Then he took her hand, still warm, in his, leaned over and kissed her good-bye.

"What's wrong, Daddy?" Lara sat in Kyle's lap on the couch, swinging her legs and staring up at him with her deep blue eyes. In her arms was a stuffed teddy bear one of the nurses at Lakeside had given her. She'd shown no interest whatsoever in her beloved Baa-Baa since the night of the attack.

He pushed a blonde curl out of her eye and hesitated. She looked so much like her mother, it was all he could do to keep from breaking down in front of her. How could he possibly tell her what she needed to know in a way she could understand?

"Daddy?" Lara tilted her head, waiting for him to answer.

He cleared his throat. "Lara, you know how Mommy's been away, that she's been sick, right?"

"I know. Mommy's been working on getting well so she can come home to us." She smiled.

Kyle shook his head, fighting back tears. "Well, honey, sometimes the doctors do all they can, and … sometimes people can't ever get well again."

Lara frowned. "Oh. Well are they going to let her come home?"

Kyle took a deep breath and held it for a moment. "No. She's not coming home."

Lara stared wide-eyed at him for a moment before bursting into tears. "Mommy's still mad at me! That's why she won't come home!" she screamed.

He held her close and stroked her hair. "No, no. That's not it."

"It is! She got mad at me and hurt me. She wants to be away from me!" Lara squirmed and tried to break away.

"No, that's not true. She loved you very much."

"Why was she so mad at me? What did I do?"

Tears streamed down Lara's beet-red face.

Kyle held her tight like a lifeline. "No, Lara. Mommy got sick." He choked back a sob. "She got sick, and that's why she hurt you, and that's why she won't be coming home."

"Will she come home someday?"

"No, baby. Not ever."

"Never again?"

"No, Lara. Never again."

"I want Mommy back!"

"I do, too, baby."

Kyle held his little girl close as she degenerated into a full-on screaming fit, eventually crying herself to sleep in his arms. Then he picked her up, the back of her little T-shirt wet with his tears, took her to her room, and gently put her in her crib.

He returned to the living room, collapsed onto the couch, and sat with his elbows on his knees and his face in his hands. His eyes and throat burned from crying along with Lara. He wasn't sure she was old enough to grasp that Mommy would never return, but he'd had to tell her something. He couldn't let her go on thinking that any day now, Mommy would come home cured.

Now that she was asleep, the place was silent except for the hum of the air-conditioning unit. Even though Gretchen had been absent for six months, it somehow seemed more empty now that she was really gone. He glanced around. Toys lay scattered all over the floor; the place was a disorganized mess. He'd paid little attention to it, other than to care for Lara, leave her with the neighbor, then go to visit Gretchen each day since she'd been admitted.

And now everything had come to an abrupt end.

Kyle knew he should call Vic and let him know. But he wasn't ready to talk to him, or anyone. He wasn't even sure he still wanted to do this work. He knew this assignment hadn't caused Gretchen's death, but his work would be forever linked in his mind with losing her. And he wasn't so sure he could handle that.

He turned out the living room lights and prepared for bed. He'd decide tomorrow.

CHAPTER 76

Tom Graham lingered in Cornucopia Technologies' break room, hoping to energize himself with a large cup of black coffee, his third of the day. He'd been up way too late again last night with a new girlfriend, and this morning he was paying the price. His eyeballs hurt like hell and he couldn't seem to concentrate.

His job bored the living shit out of him, day after dull day, so he indulged in an active nightlife to make up for it. He worked in Quality Control in the biotech food product division, and had the thrilling job of reviewing the test results for product samples. They routinely tested for purity, nutrient content, and more. He'd hoped his master's degree in biochem would have led to something more interesting, like actual product design and development, but he had to start somewhere.

Tom shrugged, downed the last of his coffee, and vowed for the hundredth time to try to do a better job. He'd slacked a bit lately and had fallen behind. He stood, stretched, and sauntered back down the hall to his workstation.

He lowered himself into his chair and rubbed at his throbbing temples. He hoped the ibuprofen would kick in soon. He flexed his shoulders and neck, took a deep breath in and let it out to try to get himself into the right frame of mind to do his work.

He tapped a few keys on his PC and pulled up the test results for a sample of Nutrio, Cornucopia's liquid food product. Stifling a yawn, he viewed the display, then stopped. He rubbed his eyes and looked again. *Can't be.* He thought they'd designed the product to avoid this problem.

But there it was. The lysine, an essential amino acid, was reversed. Just like the problem they'd had with the valine in the GMO soy last year.

Tom checked the sample's production date. *Last week.* He wasn't even caught up to the current week. But when did this start? He pulled up the test results for a sample from last month—and froze.

The lysine was reversed in that sample, too. Had he forgotten to review that batch's results, or had he missed the problem when he had? Didn't matter. Product from a month ago had long since been distributed. And consumed by millions of people. Hell, even last week's batch would have already shipped nationwide.

Tom's hands began to shake and the coffee lay sour in his stomach. He knew the implications all too well. Cornucopia was still having technical issues developing a beef product that was more three-dimensional and realistic-looking than its own SmartBeef. And SmartBeef's sales had been disappointing. But Nutrio, though the widespread brunt of jokes, had taken off. Sales were through the roof because it was convenient and affordable, and didn't taste half bad. Reversed valine had caused a public health disaster of epic proportions. Could defective lysine do the same? And what would he find if he checked the test results for a sample from *two* months ago—or longer? How long *had* the product been going out with the defective amino acid?

Sweat broke out on his forehead as Tom weighed his options. If he told anyone about the problem, he could well imagine himself being fired as Cornucopia's sacrificial lamb. But even if he did keep quiet, they rotated people around in Quality Control. Someone would eventually discover the defective lysine, figure out when it first started, and he'd be screwed anyway. And the longer it was before it was discovered, the more damage it could do. He wasn't so sure he wanted to live with that.

He turned away from his PC monitor and clapped his hands to his face as he tried to think it all through. Maybe it wouldn't cause any problems. There was no guarantee it would have the same devastating effects the defective valine did.

But it might.

Stomach churning, Tom imagined the various possible outcomes, then decided this thing was way above his pay grade. He picked up the phone to call his supervisor, Sam Taylor. Once he'd told him, he'd have done what he could. The rest would be out of his hands.

As he punched in Sam's extension, he thought of all the people who'd consumed the product—himself included—and hoped he was worried about nothing.

CHAPTER 77

"Look at *me*, Daddy! I'm a cowboy!" Lara swung one arm up in the air and rocked the brightly painted playground pony as fast as it would go.

"You sure are!"

Kyle smiled as he sat on the park bench, watching his little girl play. She'd come a long way in the last month or so. They both had. It had been a dark time, but they'd both battled back to find peace, each in their own way. Lara had finally grasped—as best a four-year-old can—that Mommy loved her very much, but would never return. Kyle nearly pulled the plug on his career in favor of a fresh start. But Dad had ruined himself by taking the blame for something he couldn't control, and he refused to fall into the same destructive pit. He'd regret scuttling a promising career in epidemiology, and it wouldn't bring back Gretchen or change anything that had happened. Nothing would.

Vic had been thrilled to have him back, and offered him a special position in the home office. He was now a team lead, guiding EIS field investigators as a sort of junior version of Vic. The job was a reward for his good work, and offered him more stability than a travel-based position so he could care for Lara.

Kyle had grown even closer to her since they'd lost Gretchen, and happily spent most of his off-hours with her. He'd brought her out to the park to play on this gorgeous Sunday afternoon in August. They had the place to themselves despite the beautiful weather.

Lara looked so much better now. Her weight was good; her eyes and hair were bright. She'd gotten the color back in her cheeks. Time, love, and good nutrition had brought back his little girl, though she would probably need plastic surgery some day to erase the ugly scar from her shoulder. She'd been so nutritionally compromised at the time of the attack that the wound hadn't healed well, leaving a twisted, angry red reminder of that horrible night.

The smile faded from his face for a moment. He missed Gretchen with all his heart, and still had to work hard to remember her the way she was *before*. Maybe that would come with time. He gazed at Lara and smiled. Her blonde curls bounced and glowed in the sun as she played cowboy and squealed with delight. She looked so much like her mother ... in better days.

"Hey, Lara! Time for a little something to eat." He reached into the soft-sided cooler he'd brought as Lara hopped off her horse and came running up to him.

"What flavor today, Daddy?" She looked up at him with bright eyes and a huge smile across her face.

"How about strawberry? I'll have some, too." Kyle pulled out two individual box containers of Nutrio, inserted the attached straws into each, and handed one to Lara. She took hers in both hands and greedily drank it down.

"Thatta girl. That's good for you, makes you strong." Kyle sipped his drink as he watched her work on hers. He didn't know how Lara would have regained her health this quickly without Nutrio.

She frowned and dropped her drink on the ground. "Daddy, my head hurts."

Kyle set his drink aside. "Maybe you drank it too fast. You know how ice cream can make your head hurt, right?"

Lara pressed her tiny hands to her temples, squeezed her eyes shut, and shrieked. "It's worse!" Her face and neck turned a purplish shade of red.

Kyle reached down and hoisted her onto his lap for a closer look. "Open your eyes, honey." He didn't like the way she was breathing in fits and starts.

Lara let out a piercing scream of terror and pain like she had that night Gretchen stabbed her. Kyle fought back the memory to focus on what was hurting her right now. "What's wrong? Where does it hurt?"

She balled her hands and shrieked as she thrashed and writhed. He struggled to hang on to her and shield his eyes from her tiny fists.

"Lara!"

As quickly as it had come, the deep red that had colored her face faded to a deathly alabaster white. She clamped her arms to her sides, hands still clenched into fists, then all her limbs stiffened straight out. She opened her mouth wide, raised her chin, and gulped another breath.

Her scream died in her throat as she went limp in Kyle's arms.

"Oh my God, Lara!"

Trembling, he gently lifted her eyelids with his fingers. Lara's sweet blue eyes were gone, consumed by pupils as wide and black as death.

Kyle rocked and moaned, clutching her still, fragile body tightly against his chest. His tears flowed down, dampening her soft blonde hair. He wept freely, suspended in a suffocating, dark grief. Nothing else existed for him until a blinding pain, solid and willful as a hammer blow, exploded inside his skull.

Kyle welcomed the release and let it take him down with Lara. He smiled up at the cloudless blue August sky before it darkened and faded away. "Lara … Gretchen …".

ABOUT THE AUTHOR

Lisa von Biela worked in Information Technology for 25 years, then dropped out to attend the University of Minnesota Law School, graduating magna cum laude in 2009. She now practices law in Seattle, Washington.

Lisa began writing short, dark fiction just after the turn of the century. Her first publication appeared in *The Edge* in 2002. She went on to publish a number of short works in various small-press venues, including *Gothic.net, Twilight Times, Dark Animus, AfterburnSF,* and more. She is the author of the novels *The Genesis Code, The Janus Legacy, Blockbuster, Broken Chain,* and *Down the Brink,* as well as the novellas *Ash and Bone, Skinshift, Moon Over Ruin,* and *Incidental Findings.*

Curious about other Crossroad Press books?
Stop by our site:
http://store.crossroadpress.com
We offer quality writing
in digital, audio, and print formats.

Enter the code FIRSTBOOK
to get 20% off your first order from our store!
Stop by today!

www.ingramcontent.com/pod-product-compliance
Lightning Source LLC
Chambersburg PA
CBHW051433170626
46809CB00006B/2444